Praise for Richard T. Ryan'

The Vatican Cameos

Winner of the Underground Book Reviews' "Novel of the Year" Award. Winner Silver Medal in the Readers' Favorite book-award contest.

"[*The Vatican Cameos* is] an extravagantly imagined and beautifully written Holmes story." – Lee Child, NY Times Bestselling author and the creator of Jack Reacher

"Once you've read *The Vatican Cameos*, you'll find yourself eagerly awaiting the next in Ryan's series." – Fran Wood, What Fran's Reading for nj.com

"Richard T. Ryan's *The Vatican Cameos* is an excellent pastiche-length novel, very much in the spirit of the original Holmes stories by Sir Arthur Conan Doyle." – Dan Andriacco, author of a host of Holmes' tales as well as the blog, bakerstreetbest.com

"Loved it! A must read for all fans of Sherlock Holmes!" – Caroline Vincent, Bits about Books

"Richard Ryan channels Dan Brown as well as Conan Doyle in this successful novel." – Tom Turley, Sherlockian author

"If you enjoy deeply researched historical fiction, combined with not one but two mystery/thriller stories, then you will really enjoy this excellent Sherlock Holmes pastiche." – Craig Copland, author of New Sherlock Holmes Mysteries

"A great addition to the Holmes Canon. Definitely worth a read." – Rob Hart, author of *The Warehouse* and the Ash McKenna series

The Stone of Destiny

"Sometimes a book comes along that absolutely restores your faith in reading. Such is the 'found manuscript' of Dr. Watson, *The Stone of Destiny*. Exhilarating, superb narrative and a cast of characters that are as dark as they are vivid. ... A thriller of the very first rank." – Ken Bruen, author of *The Guards*, *The Magdalen Martyrs,* and many other novels, as well as the creator of the Jack Taylor series

"A wonderful read for both the casual Sherlock Holmes fan and the most die-hard devotees of the beloved character." – Terrence McCauley, author of *A Conspiracy of Ravens* and *A Murder of Crows*

"Somewhere Sir Arthur Conan Doyle is smiling. Ryan's *The Stone of Destiny* is a fine addition to the Canon." – Reed Farrel Coleman, NY Times Bestselling author of *What You Break*

"Full of interesting facts, the story satisfies and may even have you believing that Holmes and Watson actually existed." – Crime Thriller Hound

"Ryan's Holmes is the real deal in [*The Stone of Destiny*]. One hopes the author is hard at work on the next adventure in this wonderfully imagined and executed series." – Fran Wood, What Fran's Reading for nj.com

"Mystery lovers will enjoy reading *The Stone of Destiny: A Sherlock Holmes Adventure* by Richard T. Ryan." – Michelle Stanley, Readers' Choice Awards

"All in all, *The Stone of Destiny* is a captivating and intriguing detective novel and another great Sherlock Holmes adventure!" – Caroline Vincent, Bits About Books

"Ryan's depictions of Holmes and Watson are impeccable, his sympathetic Irish revolutionaries are well-drawn, and his historical research is sound but not intrusive." – Tom Turley, Sherlockian author

"Richard Ryan's prose flows as easily as a stream in the summer. I thought the way the Stone was stolen, how it was transported out of England under the very noses of the army of police, and its hiding place in Ireland were brilliant!" – Raven reviews

The Druid of Death

"The clever solution, which echoes one from a golden age classic, is the book's best feature." – Publishers Weekly

"*The Druid of Death* is clever and fun, a winning combination. The setting — Victorian England — and the Druidic lore are absolutely captivating. This is my favorite kind of mystery." – Criminal Element

" … the Druidic detail and the depiction of 19th-century London are fascinating and delightful." – Kirkus Reviews

"Richard Ryan has found his niche in creating new adventures for our famous detective and his sidekick." – Caroline Vincent, Bits About Books

"*The Druid of Death* by Richard T. Ryan is a compelling story that transported me back in time and made the iconic duo of Holmes and Watson jump off the page." – Books of All Kinds

"Where many of the tangent series have been challenged to keep these characters [Holmes and Watson] fresh, this author has accomplished not only that but made them enjoyable too." – Jennie Reads

"Ryan creates a thoroughly enjoyable pastiche, giving readers just what you'd expect from such a mystery. The suspense is tangible, and the detection methodologies quirky. He's right on the money with his characterizations of all the usual players, especially Holmes and Watson." – Barbara Searles @thebibliophage.com

"A stunning achievement!" – Ken Bruen, author of *The Guards* and creator of Jack Taylor

"An excellent must-read for new and old friends of Mr. Holmes and Dr. Watson." – Terrence McCauley, award-winning author of *The Fairfax Incident* and *Sympathy for the Devil*

"*The Druid of Death*? Sign me up! Sherlock Holmes and Dr. Watson find themselves caught in a diabolical game of cat-and-mouse as the body count starts to rise. I devoured this book in an evening; you will too." – Leah Guinn, The Well-Read Sherlockian blog

"As one would expect from a Sherlock Holmes story, the Great Detective's intellect, keen eye for observation, and logical deductions all play a factor in the satisfying conclusion of this mystery." – Kristopher Zgorski, founder of BOLO Books

"Sherlockians craving a new challenge for their favorite sleuth need look no further than Richard T. Ryan's *The Druid of Death*, which puts Holmes on the trail of one of his most fiendish adversaries ever." – Steven Hockensmith, author of the Edgar Award finalist *Holmes on the Range*

The Merchant of Menace

Short-listed for the annual Drunken Druid Award.

"Oh, what a joy it is to meet Sherlock Holmes and Dr. Watson again! *The Merchant of Menace* is an exciting adventure of priceless valuables, great detective work and just the kind of devilish adversary we love to read about." – Mattias Boström, author of *From Holmes to Sherlock: The Story of the Men and Women Who Created an Icon*

"This rousing, intriguing, devilishly fun caper, well-executed and well-paced, had me hooked from the first page. The dutiful Watson, Holmes' deductive skills, and a worthy nemesis to rival the evil Moriarty himself, make this cat-and-mouse adventure a page-turning, edge-of-your-seat coaster ride well worth taking." – Tracy Clark, author of *Broken Places* and *Borrowed Time* and the creator of Cass Raines

"[In *The Merchant of Menace*], Ryan takes reality and weaves it together with Sherlockian mythology and a fun mystery." – Barbara Searles @the bibliophage.com

"[*The Merchant of Menace* is] an absolute humdinger of a novel …It is beautifully written, erudite and hugely entertaining." – Ken Bruen, the author of *The Ghosts of Galway* and the creator of Jack Taylor

"The wonderfully titled *The Merchant of Menace* has all the familiarity of a lost Holmesian tale. An enjoyable adventure from the ever reliable Richard T Ryan." – The Crime Thriller Hound

"Ryan has a real flair for capturing the language of Holmes and Watson, their foibles, and the dynamics of their relationship. He has created an antagonist and series of crimes that Conan Doyle would have been proud of." – Caramerrollovesbooks blog

"…[Holmes] encounters a rather delicious new 'villain'; this one can give Moriarty a run for his money but instead of trying to one up the brilliance of Doyle's Moriarty, Ryan pays homage in the making of his *Merchant*." – The Caffeinated Reader

"The Case, oh my, the case. This case had Sherlock stunned, but of course that just made our favorite detective work … harder. I love that the more intelligent a criminal, the more respect Sherlock has for them. This case was one of my favorites of all the Sherlock cases. It had suspense, intrigue, and surprise. The entire thing was beautifully written." – Pixie Ponders and Reviews

"With an intriguing premise and a cunning plot, *The Merchant of Menace* will delight Sherlockians of all stripes. Richard T. Ryan has given us a gripping mystery and a loving tribute to the Great Detective." – Daniel Stashower, author of *Teller of Tales: The Life of Arthur Conan Doyle*

"Deftly blending Conan Doyle and Dan Brown, Richard Ryan's *Through a Glass Starkly* offers an intriguing mix of history and mystery. Remaining true to the Canon in his depictions of the iconic Holmes and Watson, Ryan also delivers a mystery that should satisfy even the most demanding Sherlockian." – Robert Dugoni, NYT Best-selling author of *The Eighth Sister* and the creator of Tracy Crosswhite

"Ryan's Watsonian voice is superb, and as with his earlier novels the author has included several affectionate nods to the characters, stories, and intrigues of the original Canon. These twists and turns make this an engrossing and enjoyable read, as do the variety of colourful locations chosen for the action. From a secret *pied-a-terre* in Paris, to the Whispering Gallery in St. Paul's Cathedral, we are carried along at a frenetic pace. I previously read, and thoroughly enjoyed, *The Druid of Death. Through a Glass Starkly* is even better!" – Sherlock Holmes Society of London

"Mr. Ryan masterfully creates a totally engrossing and suspenseful adventure of international intrigue, kidnapping and murder." -- Wendy Heyman Marshaw, author, *Mrs. Hudson's Kitchen*

"Another brilliant addition to the Sherlock Holmes Canon" – Bruce Robert Coffin, author of the Detective Byron mysteries

"Slap on your deerstalker and grab a pipe, Richard Ryan's Sherlock Holmes strikes again. With head-scratching twists and puzzling turns, even Arthur Conan Doyle would be hard-pressed to solve thus mystery. *Through a Glass Starkly* will satisfy even the most ardent Holmes fans." – Jean M. Roberts @thebookdelight,com and the author of *The Heron*

"Richard T. Ryan does it again with *Through a Glass Starkly*. His latest pastiche featuring Sir Arthur Conan Doyle's legendary team of Holmes and Watson. Is an engrossing, twisty, delicious adventure involving a missing priceless codex, Europe on the verge of war, a mysterious woman, and shadowy figures roaming the London docks. Great fun! – Tracy Clark, author of the Cass Raines Chicago mystery series

Three May Keep a Secret:
A Sherlock Holmes Adventure

By Richard T. Ryan

Hardcover ISBN 978-1-78705-809-5
Paperback ISBN 978-1-78705-810-1
AUK ePub 978-1-78705-811-8
AUK PDF 978-1-78705-812-5

Published by MX Publishing
335 Princess Park Manor, Royal Drive, London, N11 3GX
www.mxpublishing.co.uk

Cover design by Brian Belanger.

Front cover image of The Mérode Cup by Marie-Lan Nguyen (2012).
File licensed under the Creative Commons Attribution 2.5 Generic
license. Image taken from
https://commons.wikimedia.org/wiki/File:Merode_cup_VandA_403.1_2-
1872_n01.jpg

As always this book is dedicated to my wife, Grace; as well as my daughter, Kaitlin, and her husband Daniel; my son, Michael, and his wife, Amanda,

But this is especially for my grandchildren, Riley Grace and Henry Robert.

Thank you for putting up with me!

Introduction

Three May Keep a Secret is the sixth Sherlock Holmes adventure to make its way from the battered tin dispatch box, which I acquired at an estate auction near St. Andrew's in Scotland, to the printed page.

As I have noted previously, for various reasons, all of the stories in the box apparently failed to see the light of day during Dr. Watson's lifetime. Several were politically sensitive – both in England and abroad – while others may have been perceived by Holmes as an affront to his well-known vanity. A number of the remainder might have aroused the ire of various noble and powerful families. I cannot imagine that Holmes would have been troubled in the least at the umbrage taken by others; however, Watson, being the more pragmatic of the two, would certainly have felt that discretion was the better part of valor, especially when it came to his own literary endeavors.

That being said, *Three May Keep a Secret* is a rather strange tale that may have been held back for any and all of the reasons cited above. There are certainly those moments when Holmes' brilliance is as incandescent as ever, and I believe they more than offset those rare occasions where the Great Detective is a little lagging in his usual luminescence.

However, one must also consider the possible ramifications that the revelations made in this story might have on future generations – both for the institutions, and possibly some members of the nobility – of those countries involved as well as for the common man.

Still, one cannot help but speculate what the reaction to this tale might have been had Watson chosen to reveal it over the course of several months in *The Strand.* Although I am tempted to hazard a guess, I shall refrain, since such idle speculation would almost certainly result in a reproving glance from Holmes and the recitation of one of his well-known maxims: "I never guess. It is a shocking habit — destructive to the logical faculty."

– Richard T. Ryan

Foreword

Alone and bereft of my dearest friend, I believed I had given up chronicling the adventures of Sherlock Holmes, on May 4, 1891. Like most of the rest of the world, I was under the impression that my friend had perished, along with his nemesis, Professor James Moriarty, in a fight to the death that started at the top of the Reichenbach Falls.

As you know by now, Holmes had staged his own death, and very few people knew the truth surrounding the events of that fateful day. As you are no doubt also aware, I was among those kept in the dark for three years.

During that time, I had resumed my medical practice and eschewed my pen although there were still tales to be told. I considered bringing to light a few unpublished cases, but without my companion beside me to tease and cajole me about my shortsightedness and lack of observation, it seemed rather selfish.

I consoled myself with the thought that there were other cases that I had promised to withhold for various reasons and still a few others that I had pledged would never be revealed until a set period of time had elapsed. I was optimistic about the latter affording me an excuse to resume my writing career, but in those moments of true introspection I knew I was deluding myself.

Suddenly in the spring of 1894, my world was turned upside down. Holmes had miraculously reappeared in my study disguised as an old bookseller. Shortly thereafter, Colonel Sebastian Moran was apprehended and brought to justice, and all seemed right with the world again.

Until of course, this adventure that follows began with a rather imperious note to Sherlock Holmes seeking an audience.

As fate would have it, the note was the impetus that served as a springboard to a case that required the utmost delicacy on both our parts for reasons that shall become obvious.

In the cruelest of ironies, after an extended hiatus, we at last had an adventure. I was poised – nay, I was eager – to resume my literary endeavours when fate stepped in, in the form of … I see I am getting ahead of myself. At any rate, events conspired and made it impossible for the details to be revealed at that time. As a result, my literary efforts remained stymied.

As was my wont, I wrote the case up and then assigned it to my tin dispatch box. I have no doubt that it will one day grace the pages of The Strand, and demonstrate once again the inestimable talents of my friend.

Should this particular tale have been released earlier? Perhaps. But the decision was not mine to make; after all, I had given my word. That being said and certain restrictions having expired, I offer for your consideration, the following which I have titled, *Three May Keep a Secret*.

John H. Watson, M.D.

One man may read the Bhagavata by the light of a lamp, and another may commit a forgery by that very light; but the lamp is unaffected. The sun sheds its light on the wicked as well as on the virtuous.

— Ramakrishna

"The enemy is within the gates; it is with our own luxury, our own folly, our own criminality that we have to contend."

— Marcus Tullius Cicero

"Three May keep a secret, if two are dead."

— Benjamin Franklin

Chapter 1

Of all the adventures which I have shared with my friend, Sherlock Holmes, during our years together, I am not certain that any had a more unusual beginning than that which involved the late Ralph Prescott.

The events that make up the bulk of the case began in the summer of 1894, shortly after Holmes' miraculous resurrection from the waters at the bottom of the Reichenbach Falls. As you might expect, upon his return from the "dead" and following the apprehension of Colonel Sebastian Moran, Holmes had been besieged with cases. Displaying his usual preference for the *outre,* he had refused to accept the vast majority of them, describing many of them as "mundane" or proclaiming about others that the solution was "so patently self-evident that even a Scotland Yard inspector could not fail to arrive at the correct conclusion."

One morning in late July, after I had once again taken up residence at Baker Street, I made my way home after an early morning medical emergency.

Holmes was in a fine mood, and we were chatting amicably over lunch about the violin concert he had attended the previous evening, when our long-suffering landlady knocked on our door. In his usual brusque manner, Holmes replied, "Come in, Mrs. Hudson."

She entered clutching a small envelope and said, "I am so sorry to disturb you, gentlemen, but this just arrived by messenger for you, Mr. Holmes."

Taking it from her, he opened it, and as she turned to leave, he said, "Mrs. Hudson, if you please."

After perusing it twice, Holmes looked at her and said, "Kindly inform the messenger I will not be at home at the appointed hour, and please stress I am not accepting any new cases at the moment."

"I would, sir," she replied, "but the messenger didn't wait for a reply. He simply delivered the envelope, and then he hopped on his bicycle and pedaled off toward Marylebone Road."

"Thank you, Mrs. Hudson. That will be all."

"What does it say, Holmes?"

He then handed me a single sheet of note paper, which had been folded in half. Upon opening it, I read the following:

Dear Mr. Holmes,

I shall call upon you this afternoon precisely at half three. I expect that you will make yourself available as it is a matter of some urgency – and delicacy.

I look forward to making your acquaintance.

Sincerely,

Ralph Prescott

"What do you make of it, Holmes?"

"Actually, I make rather little of it. The paper is of exceptionally fine quality and quite costly. The writer has employed a high-quality fountain pen, quite possibly a

7

Waterman or a Wirk, although I am inclined to lean strongly towards the former. The hand that composed the note is strong and confident. Further, Mr. Prescott has gone through the expense of having had it delivered by messenger service rather than post.

"I should also wager that he is an Englishman, despite the use of an American pen, given his use of the expression 'half three' rather than the more American 'half past three.'

"All of that tells me that he is a man of some means and one who is quite used to issuing orders and having them obeyed without question. I find the line 'I expect that you will make yourself available' most telling."

"A military man, perhaps?" I offered.

"Quite possibly," replied Holmes.

"Given that he declares it to be a matter of 'some urgency – and delicacy,' aren't you even the least bit curious?"

"Not at all," replied my friend dismissively. "The 'matter' – whatever it may be – is no doubt considered to be urgent and delicate by Mr. Prescott, but since I know nothing of it, I find it neither. Moreover, I have a number of pressing errands to which I must attend this afternoon."

"Oh? Do tell."

"Yes. I must visit the stationers in order to replenish my supply of paste so that I may add these articles to my indexes," he said brandishing a sheaf of papers that he had culled from the various newspapers which he devoured each morning. "Also, I need to restock my store of tobacco. Pressing business, indeed," he said, tapping the ash from his favorite briar.

"So you are not the least bit curious?"

"I have often wondered, how does one measure curiosity, Watson? Is it in bits or degrees? I have always opted for the latter, although I am certain it can be both."

At that point, I knew there was nothing to be gained in arguing with him when he had already made up his mind. Truth be told, I knew that the tone of the note had nettled my friend. Although my own sense of inquisitiveness was yearning to know more, I decided to accompany Holmes. Secretly I harbored hopes I might be able to steer him back to Baker Street in time to meet with Mr. Prescott.

After we had lunched, we set out on Holmes' "pressing errands." The afternoon began with a stop at James J. Fox on St. James Street. During the cab ride, Holmes was his usual taciturn self. However, once we arrived at the tobacconist, he became quite animated and began by purchasing enough shag to last him several weeks. Although it is a word I should never have thought to use in describing my old friend, I must say that when it came to replenishing his supply of cigarettes, Holmes positively dithered over the possibilities. Finally, after sampling more than a dozen different types of tobacco and discoursing on the merits of each, he refilled both his cigarette case and mine and purchased several dozen more for the future.

Although there was a stationery store on the next street, Holmes insisted that we must travel to Harrods, claiming that store alone carried the particular brand of paste that he preferred for his year-books. Never having known him to express any preference for paste in the past, it finally dawned upon me that my friend was trying to prolong the shopping excursion in order to avoid having to meet with Mr. Prescott.

After Holmes had concluded his performance in Harrods, I glanced at my watch and saw that it was nearing five o'clock. I said to Holmes, "I think you have accomplished your purpose."

"Oh," he remarked, the very picture of innocence, "I wasn't aware I had a 'purpose,' as you put it, aside from procuring tobacco and paste."

"Are you honestly trying to tell me there was no intent on your part to avoid your appointment with Mr. Prescott?"

"Who?" he inquired, and I almost believed him but for the slight twinkle in his eye.

"Come on, old man. I am certain he has departed by now."

So we hailed a cab and conversed about any number of subjects, from the cases he was working on to the tobacco he had just purchased to his experiments at Montpelier during his absence.

Order appeared to have been restored to the world as we stepped down from the cab in front of our lodgings. However, no sooner had we entered than Mrs. Hudson met us at the foot of the stairs.

"Oh, Mr. Holmes, Dr. Watson, I am so glad you have returned."

"Pray tell, what is troubling you, dear lady?" said Holmes.

"You had a caller, a very proper gentleman, arrive some time ago, perhaps an hour or more. Truth be told, I believe he rang the bell at exactly half three."

Holmes rolled his eyes and then said, "Yes, I was rather expecting him. I do hope you informed him of my absence and sent him on his way."

"I tried, Mr. Holmes. As God is my witness, I did."

"Tried, Mrs. Hudson? Tried? Would you care to elaborate?"

"I told 'im that you weren't in and I 'ad no idea when you'd return."

"And?" inquired Holmes.

"He nearly broke down in tears and begged me to let him wait for you. He said it was most urgent – a matter of life and death."

"Mrs. Hudson?"

"I'm truly sorry, sir. He's upstairs in your rooms. I couldn't bear to turn him away."

"You have left him alone in our rooms?"

"I waited with him much of the time, but then I had to leave in order to start preparing supper. I do hope you understand, sir."

"We shall discuss this later," said Holmes as he bounded up the stairs. I was right behind him when he threw open the door.

There sound asleep in Holmes' chair was a well-dressed man, perhaps forty-five or fifty years old. He appeared to be quite a good-looking fellow with a head of thick black hair that was beginning to grey. I could easily see how he might have charmed Mrs. Hudson. However, I knew Holmes would not be swayed.

On the table next to the man was a nearly empty decanter of brandy and a single glass.

Turning to me, Holmes seethed, "This is insufferable! This man arrives uninvited to an appointment to which I have not agreed. He then charms his way past our landlady and drinks himself into a stupor."

With that Holmes strode across the room, shook the fellow roughly by the shoulder and said, "Wake up, you rascal."

So violently had Holmes shaken him that the man toppled forward from the chair and fell on the floor face-down.

I bent over the fellow to see if he had been injured in the fall, all the while Holmes kept remonstrating – both with himself and our unconscious visitor.

Finally, he paused, looked at me and asked, "Well, just how drunk is he, Watson?"

Having finished a cursory examination, for that was all that was needed, I looked up at Holmes and replied, "He's not drunk. He's dead!"

Chapter 2

"Holmes, we must call the police immediately!"

"Not just yet, Watson," he said, bending over the body. "I should like to examine Mr. Prescott *before* we summon the authorities."

As he fished his lens from his pocket, I came to the sudden realization that Holmes finally had what he had always clamored for throughout his career, a crime scene —if indeed this were a crime – undisturbed by the various and sundry officials who would otherwise attend the discovery of a body.

Holmes was poring over the man's garments, making remarks to himself at different times – "Pick stitching … Military man, possibly a physician … Trismus … Right-handed," After he had finished his initial inspection, he began to search the dead man's pockets. Holding up a fountain pen, he exclaimed, "A Waterman, just as I suspected." After extracting the man's billfold and cataloguing the contents, he offered, "There's nearly two hundred pounds here, so I think we may safely eliminate robbery as a motive."

He continued as though I weren't there, so absorbed was he in his work, "That's rather odd."

"What is?"

"The boots," he said. "They are most definitely American."

"And you find that unusual for what reason?"

"I should think a bespoke suit from Savile Row would clamor for matching footwear, but Mr. Prescott has opted for American cowboy boots rather than English boots. Strange, very strange indeed."

I was about to remind Holmes what an individual thing taste is, but before I could even begin, he continued. "Of course, while the outer layer does provide some hints, a few of which are rather suggestive, I will not be able to form any sort of theory until we hear from the police surgeon. I do hope you will assist in the post-mortem," he said, looking up at me,

"I'd be happy to oblige if the Yard and the coroner are willing," I replied.

"Would you care to perform a more detailed examination before we summon the police?"

"If you'd like." I then bent over the man a second time and looking up at Holmes, who had now risen and was standing above us, I said, "I heard you mutter trismus as you examined him, I should also draw your attention to the facial muscles."

"Yes, the *risus sardonicus*," he replied. "I find that rather suggestive."

"Coupled with the last vestiges of cyanosis, I should say the man was poisoned."

"I quite agree," replied Holmes. "Strychnine?'

"Without having performed a proper autopsy, that would be my preliminary assessment."

Upon hearing that, Holmes nodded and smiled. "I have the feeling that the port-mortem will simply confirm what we already suspect." He then went to the door and called down to the page, "Billy, I want you to go and find the nearest constable and tell him to summon an inspector from Scotland Yard as well as the coroner."

I heard the youngster reply, "Yes sir, Mr. Holmes," and then I heard the front door slam. Holmes then returned to resume his examination, but as he continued, I could see his frustration mounting. Finally, after about 15 minutes, I heard a clamor down below and turning to Holmes, I said, "I believe the police have arrived."

"Yes, yes. Hold them at the door a second while I return everything to his pockets, will you Watson?"

I watched as Holmes pulled down the man's sleeves and trouser legs and as he went to slip the man's wallet back into his jacket pocket, I heard him say, "Hello, what have we here?"

Reaching into the pocket Holmes extracted what appeared to be a bird's feather along with a small velvet pouch. "What on Earth?" I exclaimed. "A blackbird feather? And what's in the pouch?"

"No," replied Holmes. "I think not. Given its size, I am more inclined to think this came from a raven. After all, blackbirds are smaller than crows which, in turn, are smaller than ravens. No, Watson, this most definitely came from a *Corvus corax*."

Holmes then opened the pouch and dumped five or six pieces of colored glass into his hand. He held one up for inspection and simply muttered "interesting" before returning them to the pouch and replacing the pouch in the pocket.

"What does it mean?" I asked, pointing to the feather. At that point, there was a sharp knock on the door. I watched as

15

Holmes pocketed the feather and raised his finger to his lips to indicate I should remain silent about it.

The knock on the door was repeated, and then I heard Inspector Lestrade's gruff voice, "Mr. Holmes? Dr. Watson?"

I glanced at Holmes, who nodded, so I proceeded to open the door. Stepping into our rooms, Lestrade looked at the body and said, "What have we here?"

Holmes quickly filled him in about the note and his afternoon shopping expedition and our discovery of the body when we returned from Harrods. "It's a good thing we are well-acquainted," said Lestrade, "otherwise, I might have to bring you two down to the Yard for questioning."

"You cannot be serious," I exclaimed.

"I believe the Inspector is tweaking you," replied Holmes.

I looked at Lestrade, who smiled sheepishly and replied, "I am sorry, Doctor. I certainly know you and Mr. Holmes better than that."

"Well, I should hope so," I replied tartly,

"Anything unusual about the body?" asked Lestrade.

"There is a bit of incongruity," my friend replied. Before Lestrade could reply, he continued, "The suit he is wearing appears to be new, and the pick stitching tells me that it probably came from one of the better tailors, perhaps Ede and Son in Chancery Lane. See how fine the needlework is along the lapel and the breast pocket? That is surely the work of a master tailor."

"Anything else?" queried Lestrade.

"He was probably in the military, although I cannot say for certain what country he served although I am inclined to think he was an Englishman as Mrs. Hudson, who let him in, never mentioned an accent – American or otherwise. And finally, I believe he may have been a physician."

"How did you arrive at that conclusion?" I asked, beating Lestrade to the punch.

"You see no hint of that, Watson? I am disappointed. Consider," he continued, almost as though he were a lecturer addressing two rather recalcitrant students. "The fact that he wears a wristwatch is rather telling, no? Couple that with the surgeon's cuffs on his jacket, and I should think the answer rather obvious."

That I had failed to examine the jacket closely and thus missed the surgeon's cuffs nettled me to no end.

"Watson…"

I cut Holmes off before he could finish, "I know. I see but I do not observe."

"Now, Inspector, you may remove the body. However, I would be most appreciative if you could see your way clear to let us know when the autopsy is to take place. I should certainly be in your debt."

"You suspect foul play?"

"A man sends me a note seeking my help. He arrives at my residence unbidden and then proceeds to expire in my sitting room. Come, Lestrade, even you must find that chain of events suggestive.

"Both Dr. Watson and I are of the opinion that the man died from strychnine poisoning. By the way, Inspector, I took the liberty of searching his pockets. You can rule out robbery."

"Oh?"

"There was more than two hundred pounds in his wallet. The only other thing that seems rather incongruous is the fact that he was carrying a small pouch with several bits of what appear to be colored glass in it. The pouch is in his inside jacket pocket. As a favor, Inspector, I wonder if I might be permitted to retain one of those pieces in order to study it."

"I would like to oblige you, Mr. Holmes, but they are evidence. Perhaps after everything has been examined at the Yard, I may be able to procure a piece for you to examine."

With that, Lestrade signaled to the two constables who had accompanied him, and they loaded the body onto a stretcher and removed it.

After they had departed, I could no longer contain myself. "Of all the cheek! First, he jokes that you and I might be suspects and then he refuses to let you retain a piece of glass – as if the Yard is going to know what to make of it."

When Holmes didn't respond to my outburst, I turned and found him standing by the window. He was examining something, and I was quite uncertain as to whether he had heard a single word I had said.

Finally, he turned, and I saw that he was holding a small piece of green glass. "I thought you returned all those to Lestrade."

As a smile played across his lips, he said, "I must have forgotten that I had put this piece in my pocket."

"So you have two clues to pursue," I said, "the feather and the glass."

"That is not just any plume, Watson, but rather a raven's feather. Do you not find that suggestive?"

"In what way?"

"When I say raven, what comes to mind?"

"Nevermore," I replied.

"Still reading the poems of Mr. Poe? Excellent! Anything else, perhaps a bit closer to home?"

"What are you driving at, old man?"

"I was thinking of the Tower ravens, and the prophecy regarding their residence."

"You don't mean that old superstition that holds that if the Tower of London ravens are lost or fly away, the Crown will fall and Britain with it."

"The fact that you recall it is somewhat telling. After all, my friend, I have come to regard you as a sort of Everyman."

Uncertain whether Holmes had just complimented or insulted me in some way, I remained silent.

"That you are aware of it suggests that it is rather well-known belief, and," he said, holding up the piece of glass, "and you know what is held at the Tower?"

"The Crown Jewels! Surely, you don't think …"

Holmes cut me off, "That's precisely the problem. I do not know what to think; however, I am hoping that after I consult with a few of my acquaintances on the morrow, I shall have a much clearer sense of direction."

At that point, Mrs. Hudson entered our rooms carrying a large silver tray with two covered dishes on it. "Before you do anything else, you must eat," she admonished us.

After a meal of lamb chops, roasted potatoes and spinach, Holmes retired to his chemistry table where he began to examine the glass under a microscope.

Knowing better than to disturb him during such endeavors, I dug out my volume of Poe's poems. After re-reading "The Raven," I enjoyed several other works including "El Dorado," "The Bells" and "Annabel Lee," which had become one of my favorites since my dear Mary had passed.

So immersed was I in my melancholy thoughts that I was quite startled when I heard Holmes exclaim, "Of course! It's not glass at all."

Chapter 3

"My word, Holmes, you startled me."

"My apologies, Watson. I must admit that while it is glass, at the same time, it is not," he said, holding up the small oblong that glistened like an emerald.

"You are speaking in riddles, Holmes. While I am certain that you know precisely what you mean, please try to enlighten the rest of us."

"Are you familiar with vitreous enamel?"

"Well, I am certainly familiar with the term vitreous."

"Of course, with your medical training you would be. However, I am not referring to the clear jelly that fills the eyeball, posterior to the lens; rather, I am talking about vitreous enamel."

"Would that be enamel that is glass-like?" I ventured.

"Exactly."

"So how is it glass, but not glass?"

"Vitreous enamel is actually made from powdered glass which is melted and then poured onto a surface where it is allowed to harden. The backing is then removed and you are left with something like this."

"Well that's a rather odd thing for someone to be carrying around, isn't it?"

"Indeed, it is, especially this particular type of vitreous enamel."

"I was not aware there was more than one type."

"There are several. You are perhaps familiar with cloisonné, which employs thin wires to create the outline."

"Yes, indeed. I purchased Mary a very attractive cloisonné pendant for her birthday one year." The thought of her smile when I presented it to her conjured up pleasant memories, but I was soon snatched from my reverie as Holmes continued.

"I will not bore you with the technicalities that distinguish each process, but this particular piece is an excellent example of *plique à jour*, which might be translated as 'letting in daylight.' You see how like glass it is?" he said, handing me the piece.

As I gazed through it, Holmes continued, "In *plique à jour*, the enamel is not applied to metal, but rather the enamel powder is spread over cells on a thin sheet of copper foil or mica. After it is fired and then allowed to cool and harden, the backing is then either etched away or removed with an acid solution, resulting in a stained-glass-like effect. Jewelry made with *plique à jour* often has a luminous quality because light is able to penetrate the piece from the front and back. It was quite in demand during the medieval period."

"So why was Prescott carrying several pieces and what did he wish to discuss with you?"

"Excellent questions, my friend, but at the moment, I am rather bereft of answers – a situation, as I said, I hope to remedy on the morrow. If you are not busy, perhaps you would care to accompany me."

"Nothing would please me more."

Following my surgery the next morning, I headed back to Baker Street. No sooner had I arrived than Holmes had the buttons hail a cab for us. As we climbed aboard, Holmes directed the driver to take us to the British Museum. "There is a piece I wish to examine, and perhaps I can talk to one of the curators about it," he explained as we drove.

After we had arrived, Holmes stopped at the front desk and spoke to a docent. He then headed straight for one of the galleries. His purposeful walk told me this was familiar territory for him. After perhaps five minutes, we stood in front of a glass display case that housed one of the most stunning objects I have ever seen.

Waxing eloquent, Holmes said, "Behold the Royal Gold Cup, which is also sometimes referred to as the Saint Agnes Cup."

Almost at a loss for words, I proclaimed, "It is beautiful, Holmes."

"Yes," he continued. "It is constructed of solid gold and has been lavishly decorated with pearls and enamel."

"*Plique à jour*?" I inquired.

Holmes chuckled, "No, I'm afraid not. This particular technique is known as *basse-taille*. The surfaces are engraved before the enamel is applied. Generally translucent colors are chosen that reflect light from the gold beneath."

Suddenly a deeply resonant voice interrupted Holmes, "Quite right. As for background, it was constructed for the French Royal family around the end of the 14th century. It subsequently passed into the hands of several English monarchs before languishing in Spain for nearly three centuries. The cup has a rich and varied history, and we were quite fortunate to acquire it."

I turned and saw a veritable mountain of a man. He was an inch or two taller than Holmes and quite well-built. I can only assume he must have been a rugby player in his youth. He extended a huge hand and said, "My name is Lawrence Burkhardt. I work here at the museum, and my area of expertise is the Middle Ages."

"Pleased to meet you," I said. "I am Doctor John Watson and this is –"

Cutting me off, he said, "I should think everyone in London knows Mr. Sherlock Holmes."

"You flatter me, sir," said Holmes. "Now, with regard to the cup, I believe it only recently came into the museum's possession."

"Quite right," said the man. "In fact, the museum acquired it less than two years ago, and if you can believe it, for the rather princely sum of £8,000."

"My word!" I exclaimed. "Well that would certainly explain the guard at the door."

"Yes, we cannot afford to lose such a precious treasure."

"Mr. Burkhardt," said Holmes, "since you seem to be familiar with the various processes for affixing enamel to jewelry, can you tell me how common examples of *plique à jour* are?"

"Most antiquarians hold that the process made its way from Byzantium to Western Europe, and one can find the term *smalta clara* or 'clear enamel,' which was probably intended to mean *plique à jour* in the inventory of Pope Bonifice VIII from 1295. The French term first appears in various inventories from the 14th century onwards. A full description of the process can be found in the Treatises of Benvenuto Cellini on Goldsmithing and Sculpture. It's a rather technical piece, but it should tell you everything you need to know."

"Ah yes, the *Trattato della Oreficeria*," remarked Holmes, a tad testily.

I could see my friend bristling as Burkhardt continued to wax eloquent about the subject, but perhaps he sensed Holmes' impatience, for he suddenly returned to the question that had been posed originally.

"However to answer your question, *plique à jour* pieces from the medieval period are exceedingly rare for a number of reasons. To begin with, such pieces are extremely fragile and the larger the piece of enamel the more delicate it is. Second, the technique, from everything I have learned, was quite difficult to master, so relatively few craftsmen invested their time fashioning pieces which took months to execute and quite often resulted in failure.

"Those pieces that did survive are almost exclusively small, ornamental pieces, with the best example being the Mérode Cup, from the fifteenth-century at the South Kensington Museum. It is a truly breathtaking example of craftsmanship."

"I want to thank you for your time, and I wonder if you can suggest any other authorities whose specialty is antiquities from that period."

"Certainly one possibility would be Augustus Pitt Rivers."

"Of course," said Holmes, "but isn't his real area of expertise Anglo-Saxon artifacts?"

"They are certainly his specialty," said Burkhardt, "but he has his fingers in many pies."

"And is there anyone to whom he turns when a question arises?"

"Indeed, you might also speak with Augustus Wollaston Franks. After all, it was he who acquired The Royal Gold Cup for the museum."

"Excellent," replied Holmes. "Is he available?"

"I am afraid he is out of the country at the moment. He is in Denmark, looking for pieces to add to the museum's collection."

"Well, is there anyone else?"

"I believe Madame Marianne Pittorino has returned from Italy. Although her primary area of expertise is ceramics, she is also quite knowledgeable about jewelry. She has a very small shop, almost a boutique, not too far from Hyde Park on Watt's Way, quite close to the South Kensington Museum. Here is my card, this may smooth things a bit as she can be quite guarded, but we have a very cordial working relationship."

We left the museum, hailed a cab, and some fifteen minutes later we were standing before a small shop with a sign in the window that simply said "Antiques."

As we entered, we were greeted by a young saleswoman, and Holmes asked if Madame Pittorino were available. "Whom shall I say is calling?"

Holmes smiled benignly and simply said, "My name is Sherlock Holmes and this is my associate, Dr. John Watson."

The young woman blushed and then disappeared behind some curtains. As I gazed around the store, I remarked, "These are not ordinary antiques, Holmes."

"No, I rather suspect that they should more properly be termed artifacts or antiquities."

"You are quite correct, Mr. Holmes, but people in my field know me, and the sign is merely an open invitation to the curious."

The speaker was a small, petite woman. Her dark hair framed a face that could only be described as striking. Her smile was warm and her dark eyes hinted at both intelligence and mischief. She was fashionably dressed in a costume of eggshell blue.

"Would you care to join me for some tea?" she asked, holding the curtain back and gesturing us into the back room. She led us through that room and into an office that featured floor-to-ceiling bookshelves. As she prepared the tea, my eyes took in cups, vases, busts and jewelry of all types.

"I keep my most valuable possessions in this room," she said, following my gaze. "The windows are secured with steel shutters at night, and I sleep above the shop with a loaded revolver in the top drawer of my nightstand."

I wondered if she had ever had occasion to use it but decided to refrain from asking.

Holmes began, "I understand you are somewhat of an expert on medieval jewelry."

"Pray tell, who has been telling tales out of school?"

"Mr. Lawrence Burkhardt suggested I contact you."

"That certainly puts things in a different light. As I am sure Mr. Burkhardt informed you, I am sometimes consulted when the authenticity of a piece is in question. However, as I am also sure you are aware, there are others who perform the same service."

"And do you do that sort of work often?" he asked.

"More than you might suspect, Mr. Holmes."

"Would you care to elaborate?"

"While museums are constantly seeking to augment their collections and willing to pay handsomely to do so, there are any number of unscrupulous individuals willing to part museums from their funds for nothing more than a cleverly constructed forgery. You might be surprised to learn that there are probably more fakes on the market than genuine artifacts."

"That would not surprise me in the least," replied Holmes. Reaching into his pocket, he extracted his handkerchief, unwrapped it and handed her the green glass which he had pocketed the day before. "May I ask your opinion of this particular piece?"

Taking the glass, she produced a jeweler's loupe from her desk drawer and went to the window where the light was better. After a minute or two, she turned to us and said, "Given the texture and craftsmanship, this is obviously of modern construction; however, if it were set in a piece, such as a cup or a chalice, it would be impossible to tell that it was not genuine."

"Why is that?" asked Holmes.

"In order to verify that this piece was not authentic, you would have to remove it from the article in question. Such a process could easily damage the object and once out, you might never to be able to reset it properly. Also, you run the considerable risk of having the enamel shatter."

Returning the glass to Holmes, she continued, "Would you run the risk of destroying a piece of history on a mere supposition? Perhaps someday, science will advance to the point where we can easily discern the fakes. However, for the present, I can assure you gentlemen that any number of objects on display in museums and private collections around the world – were they to be properly examined – would be found wanting when it comes to their provenance."

Chapter 4

Holmes paused to consider the weight of her words. "So if I understand you correctly," he said holding up the green glass, "this piece of glass was probably constructed in order to enhance a bogus artifact?"

"Given, its shape and size, I can see no other possible use for it," she replied. "May I ask how you happened to come by it?"

Holmes ignored her question and continued along his own path, "And I can assume that any such artifact employing this particular technique would command a fairly significant price?"

"Indeed. Since you spoke with Mr. Burkhardt, I can assume you know what the British Museum paid to obtain the Royal Gold Cup. If another such piece were to come on the market, it could command a similar price and if it featured *plique à jour,* perhaps the rarest goldsmithing technique of the Middle Ages, I can assure you that the bidding could easily pass £10,000 – especially if it were to go up for sale at an auction."

"My word," I exclaimed.

"Yes, Doctor, and depending upon the artifact in question, £10,000 could be a conservative estimate."

"How many such objects might be found in museums in London?" I asked.

"Just one," she replied, "the Mérode Cup,"

"We were planning to see the Mérode Cup after we had finished our conversation with you," Holmes said.

Madame Pittorinio smiled at him and said, "Someone has been brushing up on his medieval artifacts."

"Not at all, I assure you. I remember reading about the cup as a youngster, and as Watson will attest, I am an omnivorous reader with a strangely retentive memory for trifles – not that one could ever consider the Mérode Cup, a trifle. I have also visited the museum several times since its acquisition."

"Why don't you tell me what you know, Mr. Holmes, and I will fill in any blanks when you are finished. It will save me the time of informing you of things of which you are already aware."

I could see Holmes appreciated the woman's directness, and so he began, "I believe the cup was produced sometime around the beginning of the fifteenth century. If memory serves, there is some dispute regarding its provenance – compounded by the fact that the cup is unmarked – with some experts claiming it is French while others opt for Flanders and still others believe it to be of German origin.

"I know that it is constructed of silver, silver gilt and gold and that it has come to be regarded as the standard early example of *plique à jour*."

"Bravo, Mr. Holmes," she exclaimed, and I could see that he was touched by that slight bit of flattery.

"As to the cup's more recent history, I leave that to you Madame."

Without consulting notes of any sort, she began, "In 1872, Mr. Edward Paul wrote a memo. In it he stated: 'This curious cup was purchased by the grandfather of the present owner in the year 1828 at The Hague from the Comte de Mérode, in whose family it had been handed down for several generations. It was supposed to be a unique specimen . . .' As you may know, Mr. Paul's grandfather was the collector Henry Bevan."

I know I was impressed by her command of the subject and from the expression on his face, I believe Holmes was as well.

She continued, "The Comte de Mérode, from whom he bought the beaker, has not been identified, but was presumably either Charles-Guillaume-Ghislain or one of his sons – Henri, Félix, Frédéric or Werner. While still in Bevan's collection it was described by Henry Shaw simply as 'a German beaker of the fifteenth century.' Shaw goes on to state that 'it was bought by Mr. Bevan at Antwerp many years ago and is no doubt of Flemish workmanship.' This contradicts Paul's record as to its provenance, but the difference is of little significance, since in 1828 The Hague was the capital of the United Kingdom of the Netherlands.

"In June 1862, the beaker was exhibited as the property of Mrs. Paul at the special exhibition of works of art of the Medieval, Renaissance and more modern periods at the South Kensington Museum.

"Although some doubts regarding its authenticity have arisen during the second half of the century, they were quickly dismissed since the style and provenance of the piece, its date of acquisition by Bevan and the condition of the enamels are alone sufficient to guarantee its authenticity."

"I assume you were one of those defending the cup's authenticity," Holmes stated.

"Having seen the cup yourself, I am certain you will find that my efforts on its behalf were not misplaced."

After we had concluded our business and stepped outside the shop, Holmes said, "If we hurry, we should be able to spend a fair amount of time at the museum and perhaps elicit the opinion of another expert. Although I must admit, I am inclined to trust Madame Pittorino's judgment; she is a remarkable woman."

We walked along Watt's Way, which became Princes Gate, and then turned left on Exhibition Road. As we approached the entrance, I saw a familiar face on the steps. Before I could say anything, Holmes said, "I never thought of Lestrade as a culture maven."

At that moment, the little detective, who had been standing between the two doors, spotted us and started walking towards us. When we met, he looked at us, but spoke to Holmes and said, "Well, you certainly took your time getting here."

"How on Earth did you know where to look, Inspector? I must say I am impressed."

Lestrade smiled slyly and said, "Need I remind you that you are not the only detective in London,. Mr. Holmes."

"No, it would appear not. To what do we owe this honor, Lestrade?"

"There has been another murder, and I thought you might like to accompany me to the crime scene?"

"I am always interested in murder, Lestrade, but what makes this one so singular that you sought out my help before you have even begun to investigate?"

"The dead man, one Chester Boles, is a goldsmith of no small repute."

Although he tried to mask it and probably did succeed in hiding his feelings from Lestrade, I could tell that Holmes had been taken aback by the Inspector's revelation.

"Well I must say, that is twice in one day that you have surprised me, Lestrade, Will wonders never cease!"

Lestrade had a cab waiting, and after we had clambered aboard, the Inspector gave the driver an address on Leather Lane in Hatton Garden. During the ride, Lestrade explained the police surgeon who was to examine Prescott's body had a brother who was a jeweler. He had summoned his brother to the Yard and shown him the glass pieces. After examining them, he had opined that they were probably intended to adorn a piece of jewelry."

"That still doesn't explain why you contacted me, nor how you knew to wait for us at the Museum."

"As for contacting you, I shouldn't be surprised if I were to search you to discover that you have a small piece of that glass on your person."

Holmes glanced at me but said nothing.

Lestrade continued, "With regard to the museum, as you like to say, Mr. Holmes, if I were to explain it to you, you might not think as highly of my abilities as you do now, so do let me enjoy it a bit longer. It doesn't happen very often that I am one up on you."

I could see that Holmes was nettled, but he graciously allowed the Inspector to savor his moment in the sun. Holmes then lapsed into silence, and I am certain that he was bringing all his faculties to bear on ascertaining exactly how Lestrade had discerned our whereabouts and how he had divined that Holmes had kept a piece of the glass.

A few moments later we pulled up in front of a shop on Leather Lane. The sign above the door read – C. Boles, Jeweler – in fancy script. A burly constable had been stationed outside the door with another man who appeared to be visibly overwrought. As we approached, the constable nodded to Lestrade and said, "No one has gone in nor out, just as you instructed sir. I've asked Mr. Willoughby here to remain, but as you can see, he is quite upset."

"Well, he can be upset a while longer. I want Mr. Holmes to examine the scene before the rest of the investigators trample all over everything." Turning to Holmes, Lestrade said, "That is what you would prefer, is it not?"

"Thrice in one day. Lestrade. I am beyond amazed!"

We entered the shop with Lestrade leading the way. It was a rather small business, with glass-fronted display cases, forming a large U-shape. Several of the displays appeared to have been rifled as they were in a state of disarray. Holmes paused to examine the cases and the items that remained. From what I could discern, the items left appeared to be high quality jewelry and watches.

Lestrade led us through a doorway into a back room which also doubled as a workroom. There were two tables set up with various tools spread out along each. There was also a large safe along one of the walls. In the corner was a roll top desk, which was cluttered with papers and other paraphernalia. Sprawled awkwardly on the floor in front of the desk was the body of a man. From what little I could see of his face, he appeared to be in his late fifties or early sixties. Gesturing to the body, Lestrade said, "That is, or perhaps I should say was, Mr. Chester Boles. He owned this store, and was apparently highly regarded as a craftsman."

The man was lying face down and his white shirt and dark blue waistcoat were stained with crimson splotches. There were several jagged holes in the waistcoat where he had quite obviously been stabbed. Holmes bent over the body, pulled his glass from his pocket and began a careful examination.

"I assume that Willoughby fellow discovered the body," said Holmes.

"Yes," replied Lestrade. "He had gone out to make a delivery. Since Boles was afraid of being robbed, he was in the habit of closing the store when he was alone. He would reopen when Willoughby returned."

"Well, robbery certainly wasn't the motive for the murder," said Holmes. "Although the counters at the front of the establishment appear to have been ransacked, many of the pieces that remain are quite valuable. No self-respecting thief would leave that kind of loot behind. Watson, be a good fellow and see if that safe is locked."

I walked over, pulled on the handle, and the door swung open soundlessly on well-oiled hinges.

Holmes merely looked at Lestrade, smiled and returned to his examination of the body. "He obviously knew and trusted his attacker," said Holmes.

"Because he turned his back on him?" I ventured.

"Exactly," replied Holmes, who had risen and was now examining the workmen's tables. Bending closer, he moved from one table to the other and back several times. Finally, he said, "Our killer did not come here with the intention of murdering Mr. Boles, and since we have already eliminated robbery, all that remains is some sort of disagreement that turned violent."

"Not so fast, Mr. Holmes," Lestrade said. "Perhaps our attacker followed Boles into this back room, stabbed him and then took what he could carry and bolted."

"I don't think so, Lestrade, but if that is the line you wish to pursue, by all means follow your instincts."

"I'm not saying you are wrong, Holmes, I was merely proposing another possibility."

"Then I will give you some certainties, Inspector. I have little doubt that our killer is right-handed, powerfully built and perhaps six feet tall – give or take an inch."

"And how did you determine that?" inquired Lestrade.

"The wounds are angled from the right side. He appears to have held Boles around the neck with his left arm and hand while stabbing repeatedly with his right. The wounds also appear to have been delivered on a plane. He wasn't stabbing up nor down, which would make him approximately the same height as Boles. Finally, I believe Boles was killed using a jeweler's punch. Both sets of tools on these benches are identical, but the one on the left is missing a punch. The end of the punch is not particularly sharp which is why I say our killer was powerfully built.

"To stab a man repeatedly with a less than sharp implement does require considerable strength. Now, I should like to talk to that fellow, Willoughby, but let's do it in the front room. No point in subjecting him to the sight of this more than need be."

Lestrade had the constable bring the assistant jeweler inside, and his face was still ashen. Before leaving, the constable said to Lestrade, but loud enough so that we could all hear, "His story checks out, Inspector."

"Mr. Willoughby," Lestrade began, "after you made your delivery, you returned here straightaway?"

"Yes sir," replied Willoughby. "I had to travel to St. James Wood to deliver a brooch to Lady Esterly. The clasp had broken and Mr. Boles repaired it yesterday. I believe she planned to wear it to a special occasion this very evening."

"Approximately how long were you away?" asked Holmes.

"Just about two hours,"

"And when you returned, did you notice anything amiss?"

"Yes sir, the door was unlocked. Mr. Boles never leaves the door unlocked when he is in the shop by himself. I thought it queer, but then I thought he might have opened it for some special customer. When I entered the shop and saw the cases, I knew something was terribly wrong. I then ran into the back room where I saw the body. Then I came outside and started yelling for a constable."

"Excellent," said Lestrade. Looking at Holmes, he said, "Do you have any questions, Mr. Holmes."

"I have several, but let me start with this one. Exactly how much was Mr. Boles in debt?"

Chapter 5

"Why, what on earth do you mean?" Willoughby spluttered. "Mr. Boles didn't owe anyone anything."

Holmes looked at him and said, "I assure you this will go much more smoothly for everyone involved if you tell me the truth." Then raising his voice just slightly and adopting a tone I had only heard him use a few time in all our years together, he looked at Willoughby and stated, "I am your only chance at survival, but if you lie to me again, I will not protect you."

The change in the jeweler was astonishing. "He liked to gamble," Willoughby said. "He was especially fond of the horses. Since he was a jeweler, the touts figured he was good for the money. But he just kept losing and losing. Finally he was in danger of losing the shop and everything in it as well as his home when about seven or eight months ago a gentleman walked in one afternoon and asked to speak to Mr. Boles.

"They went into the back room, and I couldn't hear much of what they said, but after that day, Mr. Boles was a much happier man. That's all I can tell you."

"This gentleman," said Holmes, "has he returned to the shop since that first occasion?"

"Indeed, he has sir. He has been in to speak with Mr. Boles every two or three weeks since then. Whenever he arrived, they would go into Mr. Boles' office, all the way in the back, and close the door, so I couldn't hear anything that was said."

"Can you describe this gentleman?" asked Holmes.

"I would say he was perhaps forty-five or fifty. He looked to be quite fit. He was always well-dressed, and he had a head of dark hair that was just beginning to gray at the temples."

"Well that certainly narrows things down," remarked Lestrade, his voice dripping with sarcasm.

"If you saw him again, you would recognize him?" Holmes asked.

"Yes, sir. I certainly would,"

"Can you recall anything else about this man," Holmes prodded. "Perhaps a distinctive ring or a tie pin that caught your eye?"

"Nothing like that," he replied, but then suddenly his face lit up. "One time when I was coming back from lunch, he came out of the shop and flagged down a hansom. I heard him tell the driver to take him to the Northumberland Hotel."

"Well that is a place to begin," remarked Holmes. "Thank you, Mr. Willoughby. If you should think of anything else, please contact either Inspector Lestrade or myself," Holmes said as he handed the man his card.

As I prepared to hail a cab, Lestrade joined us. "By the way," the Inspector began, "the post mortem on that chap who died in your flat is scheduled for 10 o'clock tomorrow morning at University College Hospital, should you care to attend."

Holmes looked at me, "Are you free, Watson?"

I nodded, and then Holmes said to Lestrade, "Certainly one of us, perhaps both, will be there. Until tomorrow, Inspector."

As we rode in the cab, I said to Holmes, "How did you tumble to the fact that the dead jeweler was in debt?"

"Simplicity itself," he remarked. "When I examined the body, I noticed there were circles on the ring fingers of both hands, indicating he had worn rings for a long period of time, but no longer. Either he had sold them or put them up for sale, perhaps in his own shop. I'm inclined to the former as he no doubt needed the cash in a hurry to stave off his creditors."

"That just means he no longer wore his rings. Perhaps his hands had swollen."

Holmes waved away my objection dismissively. "Couple that with the fact that he was using a trained jeweler to deliver packages, and we have a man too pressed for funds to hire a delivery service."

"And you knew Willoughby was a trained jeweler instead of just a clerk?"

"There were two workmen's tables as well as two full sets of tools and two aprons." With that he smiled at me and lapsed into silence.

After we had arrived at Baker Street, Holmes changed into his blue dressing gown and began to pull his various yearbooks from the shelves. As he sat there, Mrs. Hudson brought up dinner.

I told her, "He's concentrating. I'm certain, he will take some nourishment in a little while."

After settling myself at the table, I said to Holmes, "This is a delicious looking piece of beef. Are you sure you won't join me." I was answered by silence, so I finished my meal and poured myself an after-dinner brandy. I considered offering one to Holmes, but refrained, knowing my proposal would be rebuffed.

By this time, he was loading his pipe again, and the room was becoming stuffy, so I decided to head to my club. I spent a pleasant evening playing cards and even managed to win a few quid.

When I returned home shortly after ten, I found Holmes much as I had left him although the room was now filled with smoke. After opening one of the windows, I headed off to bed, simply saying, "Good night, Holmes," as I passed.

The next morning at breakfast, Holmes was still in a dour mood. Having remained silent for so long, I decided to beard the lion in its den, "Out with it, old man. What is the matter?"

"I am failing, Watson."

"You don't mean because Lestrade knew where to find us?"

"No, that was child's play once I gave it a moment's thought." Before I could interrupt and ask him to explain, he continued, "We have two dead bodies – one of which *we* discovered, and I have virtually nothing to go on. I am certain that the deaths of Prescott and Boles are connected. I should think a blind man could see that, but as things stand, I have no clues to follow. All we have is a raven's feather and a vague description of a man in his forties or fifties, who may or may not have been a guest at the Northumberland."

"Perhaps the post mortem will shed some light on the cause of Prescott's death," I ventured.

"One can but hope, old man." Glancing at his watch, Holmes said, "We should have time for one more cup of coffee before we set out for University College Hospital."

So it was that fifteen minutes later, we were in a cab rolling along Marylebone Road. As we passed through Park Square, Holmes suddenly sat bolt upright. "I wonder," he said aloud, and then lapsed back into silence, lounging against the seat until we had reached the hospital. At that point, he threw open the door, jumped down from the cab, tossed a coin to the driver and said to me, "Come along, Watson. We have important work to do."

A short while later we were in the basement of the hospital where we met Lestrade and Dr. Brian Fairlie, who was preparing to finish the post mortem on Ralph Prescott. I was acquainted with Fairlie and knew that he was highly regarded among our profession. A tall, slender Irishman, Fairlie had been a few years ahead of me in medical school.

He greeted Holmes and me, saying, "It has been quite a while since I last saw you, Dr. Watson. I imagine your association with Mr. Holmes has curtailed your practice to some degree." Uncertain how to respond, I merely nodded.

"I had no idea you were coming," Fairlie continued, "and since I had to be in early, I simply finished up that work and then came down here to begin. As you might have surmised, there are definite traces of strychnine in both the stomach and the liver. I tried three different reagents – all yielded the same result."

"Watson and I rather suspected that to be the case," Holmes said drily. "Was there anything else noteworthy?" asked Holmes.

"I should think so," replied Fairlie. "The man has lost his right leg and was wearing something very close to a Hanger Limb." Reaching beneath the sheet that covered the body, he extracted a wooden leg that ran from the knee down and featured a crudely formed foot that had been attached by a hinge of some sort. It was perhaps three feet long.

"A Hanger Limb?" asked Lestrade.

"Yes," Fairlie said, "It is a prosthesis, an artificial leg if you will, made from barrel staves and metal. This one, like the original, on which it was modeled, features hinged joints at the knee and ankle."

"Blimey," said Lestrade, "I've only seen the peg-legs that sailors on the docks use."

"It was invented during the American Civil War, by one James Hanger, who fought for the Confederacy. At the moment, the Hanger Limb is the most advanced limb in the history of prosthetics," said Holmes, adding, "Well, that explains the cowboy boots."

"Yes, but this leg was even more special," offered Fairlie.

"Oh?" inquired Holmes.

"The area from the knee to the ankle had been padded, and it could obviously be used to conceal small items."

"Perhaps Prescott was a smuggler of some sort," I exclaimed.

"That may well be," replied Fairlie.

"Was there anything concealed in the secret compartment?" asked Lestrade.

"Just two pieces of paper," said Fairlie as he reached into the leg and extracted them. He intended to hand them to Lestrade, but Holmes intercepted them and was poring over them intently while Lestrade stood by idly, doing his best to keep his temper in check.

Finally, Holmes passed them to Lestrade who examined them. After a moment, he looked at Holmes and said, "Well, these seem harmless enough – a drawing of a cup of some sort, with some numbers below it, and I can't quite tell what this other thing might be."

However his words seemingly fell on deaf ears, for Holmes was now examining the artificial leg with his lens. Watching him pore over each section of the leg, I was struck, as I often am, by how much he reminded me of a fine hunting hound which has suddenly picked up the scent. I glanced at Lestrade who merely shrugged his shoulders. He, too, was familiar with my friend's unorthodox methods and knew better than to disturb him when he was in such a mood. After several minutes, Holmes suddenly said, "Halloa! What have we here?"

Turning, he showed us how a portion of the heel had slid out. Holding the leg in one hand, I saw Holmes holding a piece of clear glass in his other.

"Why would he hide a piece of glass in the heel?" I asked.

"This isn't glass," said Holmes. "It's a diamond."

.

Chapter 6

Lestrade then said, "That's evidence, Mr. Holmes."

"Of course it is," replied my friend.

As he handed the stone to Lestrade, he deftly retrieved the papers that had been concealed in the leg. Taking them from the Inspector, Holmes said, "Would you mind if I held onto these, Inspector? I have a few other avenues I should like to pursue, and these may prove quite helpful."

"Well just be careful with them, Mr. Holmes. After all, they could prove to be crucial pieces of evidence and they may need to be produced." He then began to examine the stone. "It's not bright and shiny like a diamond."

"It is a diamond nonetheless, and unless I miss my guess, it may prove to be quite valuable and extremely important to this case."

"This thing?" Lestrade replied. "How could it be important when no one even knew he had it?"

"That is precisely the point, Inspector. So do take proper care of it."

"And you take care with those papers," was Lestrade's retort.

"I shall guard them with my life," replied Holmes as he handed them to me. "Hold on to these, will you, old man? I need to examine the body a bit more carefully."

Donning a pair of gloves, Holmes then employed his lens as he inspected the head and then the entire body. What exactly he was looking for, I had no idea, but his occasional grunts told me he had discovered one or two points of interest. After he had finished, he thanked Dr. Fairlie and said, "I think I have seen everything I need here. Are you still in possession of Mr. Prescott's clothing?"

"I have it right here," replied Fairlie, who reached under the table and extracted a metal basket. I recognized the suit that Prescott had been wearing as well as the rather distinctive cowboy boots. Holmes immediately began to examine the boots, turning them over and paying particular attention to the sole and heel.

When he had finished, he turned to Lestrade and said, "Inspector, we now have two murders, and unless I am mistaken, they are linked, so do be careful. However, don't let that take away from your lunch with Assistant Commissioner Brooks at Goldini's. Do give him my best."

"How in heaven's name?" spluttered Lestrade.

However, Holmes was already striding through the doors, ignoring Lestrade's protestations. I trailed behind, shaking my head in bewilderment and when I finally caught up, Holmes said, "We will see how the good Inspector likes it when the shoe is on the other foot."

When we had left the hospital and secured a cab, Holmes instructed the driver to take us to the South Kensington Museum. Inside the cab he was almost jubilant, if such a term could ever be applied to Holmes.

"Obviously, you have made some progress," I said.

"Indeed, that artificial leg was a veritable font of information, and the presence of a diamond is most suggestive. After all, how many men could afford such a prosthesis, and we now know that was an imitation Hangar Limb, probably made in this country, so I should think we are well on our way to identifying the mysterious Mr. Ralph Prescott."

"And now we are on our way to examine the Mérode Cup?" I ventured.

"Indeed, and the most satisfying part of doing it this morning is that I can guarantee we won't find Lestrade waiting for us on the front steps," he said.

By way of reply, I said, "I suppose you are feeling vindicated having turned the tables on the Inspector."

"Not vindicated, Watson, so much as disappointed in myself that I didn't see the solution sooner."

"I'm still not seeing it, so perhaps you would care to enlighten me?"

"Come now, you were with me the entire time. Do give it some thought, and I am certain that you will arrive at the same conclusion as I."

"In the interim will you at least tell me how you knew Lestrade was meeting Assistant Commissioner Brooks at Goldini's?"

"The solution to that is even simpler than the riddle posed by Lestrade anticipating our whereabouts yesterday."

"You don't say?"

"Brooks owes me more than a few favors, so I contacted him last night, while you were at your club, and I arranged for him to invite Lestrade to lunch. I simply requested he leave my name out of it entirely."

"Holmes, you are incorrigible."

"Now, I believe you had voiced the prospect that given the secret compartment in his leg that Prescott might be working as a smuggler. That is certainly a possibility and a very plausible one, my friend. However, unless he were smuggling gems, which he may well have been, he couldn't conceal a great deal of contraband in that leg, so I am more inclined to think that Prescott was a courier of some sort. After all, he had a fairly detailed drawing of the Mérode Cup as well as a second sketch of a plate or platter of some type."

"I believe Lestrade also mentioned numbers below the cup."

"Possibly dimensions or perhaps a code of some sort. Once I examine them more carefully, I will know better. That is the main reason why I asked Lestrade if I might hold the papers."

"And the secondary reason?"

"Secondary reason?"

"Come, Holmes. I have known you far too long. When you make such seemingly innocent requests, quite often there are multiple reasons for your actions, and the blasé manner in which you swore to Lestrade you would guard them with your life and then passed them to me serves only to underscore my point. They are obviously quite important, but you didn't want Lestrade to know that."

"I have said it before, I will never quite get your measure, Watson. As for the secondary reason, I need time to try to identify the other object in the sketch. As I said, it appears to be a plate or platter, but the drawing is detailed enough that I am quite hopeful about identifying it and then locating it – if it is to be found."

"What do you mean, 'if it is to be found?'"

I received no answer to my question as we had arrived at the museum and Holmes was already outside the cab, handing a note to the driver.

We entered the museum, which had opened some forty years earlier and grown considerably since then. We made our way to the Medieval and Renaissance Gallery, and there I caught my first glimpse of the Mérode Cup. The cup itself was surprisingly small, perhaps four inches tall, but it is a truly stunning piece of craftsmanship. Next to it sat the cover, which was perhaps three inches tall by itself. The detail work on both pieces was breathtaking, and the translucent enamel panels on both glistened like so many miniature stained glass windows.

"You can see why the piece is so highly regarded," remarked Holmes. "It is too bad they cannot illuminate it properly. Still, this new display case – it has changed significantly since I last saw it a year before my unexpected demise – and the enhanced lighting, even in this rather dreary setting, speak to the genius of man. It truly is one of a kind."

"Unless, of course, someone makes another," I joked.

Holmes peered at me, and I found the expression on his face rather difficult to decipher. After a few seconds, he returned his gaze to the cup and then a few seconds after that he simply said, "My thoughts exactly, Watson."

After perhaps thirty minutes in the museum, during which Holmes looked to see if he could find any items that matched the other drawing, he gave up and we returned to Baker Street. No sooner had we entered our rooms than Holmes pulled out one of his yearbooks and began perusing each page carefully. Shortly after that, Mrs. Hudson brought up lunch, and she encouraged Holmes to eat.

He submitted to her wishes reluctantly, and had just sampled the soup, which he pronounced, "Excellent!" much to her delight, when I heard the front door bell ring.

Mrs. Hudson left to answer the door and a few minutes later returned with a rather distinguished looking gentleman in tow. She introduced him saying, "This is Mr. Vito Lasalandra, from the International Fine Arts Commission."

He bowed and Holmes said, "I am Sherlock Holmes and this is my associate, Dr. John Watson. How may I be of assistance?"

"You come highly recommended, Mr. Holmes, from many quarters," he replied in flawless English.

"Thank you," said my friend, "it is always nice to know that one's work is appreciated, but that still doesn't answer my question."

"I see that you waste no time; I like that in a man. My job, Mr. Holmes, is twofold. On one hand, I am tasked with recovering those *objects d'art* that have been looted from various cities throughout Italy. At the same time, I make it my solemn duty to bring to justice all those who would defraud museums and collectors by offering items for sale, usually on the black market, which have little or no historical value, but which might fool even the most seasoned collector."

"And what exactly is it you would like from me, Mr. Lasalandra?"

"I need your help. Before I proceed, I must be assured of your absolute discretion."

"Given my reputation, I should think such an assurance would not be necessary," replied Holmes rather coolly.

At that Lasalandra glanced at me, as Holmes continued, "I can assure you that anything you wish to say to me may be said in front of Dr. Watson. He is the very soul of circumspection."

Lasalandra nodded, seemingly satisfied, and continued, "As science advances, the tools for creating forgeries continue to improve. I am sure you are aware that in museums all over the world there are any number of items – paintings, statues, artifacts – being exhibited that are, in fact, little more than clever copies.

"It is a plague because museums are bilked out of enormous sums and augmenting their collections with items that are worth only a pittance of what was paid for them."

"I fail to see how this involves me," replied Holmes.

"Several years ago, I found myself tracing the provenance of a small reliquary the Vatican Museum wished to purchase. During my investigation, I encountered an American, George Grey Barnard, living in Moret-sur-Loing, just south of Paris. He had studied at the Academie des Beaux-Arts in Paris and achieved some renown as a sculptor."

At that point, Holmes coughed rather pointedly. Lasalandra looked at him and said, "You want to know where this is going? Barnard began to deal in 13th- and 14th-century objects as a means to supplement his income and provide for his family. He had also amassed a rather enviable personal collection. He began by buying and selling stand-alone objects with various French dealers, but then he began to acquire *in situ* architectural artifacts from local farmers. At the same time he discovered that there was a thriving market in counterfeits. After he had proved that several objects purchased by a rather well-known museum, which propriety forbids me from naming, were bogus, he began to find himself in demand as a consultant.

"He and I formed an alliance of sorts. I resigned my position with the Vatican and went to work with Barnard. Before long, we along with several other like-minded individuals from around the world, had joined forces, and the work was constant. We were employed by the Louvre, the American Museum of Natural History as well as the Uffizzi and several others."

"You still haven't told me why you need my help," said Holmes.

"One of our most trusted members has gone missing, and it is imperative that we locate him."

"How long has he been missing?" asked Holmes.

"We last heard from him five days ago."

"His name?"

"Robert Priestley, although when he was working among the counterfeiters, pretending to be one of them, he would sometimes use the name Ralph Prescott."

Chapter 7

Holmes shot me a look before I could say anything. "You say you last heard from your associate five days ago?"

"Yes. He wired me to say he was in London. Although his telegram was rather cryptic, I believe he was attempting to track down a new scientific process."

"That's rather vague," observed Holmes.

"He had originally been sent here because we have been seeing a large number of gold bracteates offered to museums in several countries recently."

"Bracteates?" I inquired.

Holmes looked at me and said, "A bracteate is a flat, thin, single-sided gold medal, often worn as jewelry. If memory serves, they were produced in Northern Europe predominantly during the Migration Period of the Germanic Iron Age. Although I do believe they date all the way back to the Persians."

"You have it exactly, Mr. Holmes."

"Is there anything distinctive about this new batch of bracteates?"

"Many of them bear the image of Odin, along with Huginn and Muninn perched on his shoulders."

"That might help to explain the feather you discovered in Prescott's pocket," I blurted out.

Both Lasalandra and I stood there in silence. I knew why I was confused; however, I could not venture to say what was puzzling our Italian visitor.

Finally, Lasalandra said, "I think I deserve some sort of explanation, Mr. Holmes."

Holmes then proceeded to fill in the Italian about the note and the missed appointment, glossing over the fact that he had deliberately dallied in order to avoid having to deal with Prescott. He also mentioned the papers in the prosthesis but neglected to mention they were in his possession, nor did he bring up the diamond he had discovered in the heel. Finally, he omitted the murder of the jeweler, Chester Boles.

When he had finished his rather sketchy recitation, he said to Lasalandra, "Have you any idea what type of process Prescott may have been looking into?"

"I cannot say exactly, but I am certain that it has something to do with producing bogus pieces of jewelry which are being passed off as antiques."

"I am inclined to agree with you," said Holmes. "May I suggest that you pursue your avenues of investigation while I follow mine? Perhaps, we can meet in a few days' time to see what progress we have made."

"Excellent, Mister Holmes. I am staying at the Savoy, Room 402. I look forward to hearing from you."

With that he shook our hands, bowed and took his leave.

After he had left, I apologized to Holmes profusely for my slip of the tongue.

"These are treacherous waters, Watson. Mr. Lasalandra may be exactly who he says he is, but he may also be someone else entirely. I think for the moment we will play this hand quite close to the vest. You must try to be a bit more judicious in the future."

"I know the things you omitted telling Lasalandra. You don't trust him?"

"I don't know him, so I cannot trust him – yet. That may change, we shall see."

After a rather awkward silence, I changed the subject, asking simply, "Huginn and Muninn?"

"In Norse mythology they were ravens, Watson, who sat perched on Odin's shoulders. If memory serves, Huginn would be translated as 'thought' while Muninn would be the equivalent of 'memory' or 'mind.' In a very real sense, they were Odin's eyes and ears as they would fly all over the world and bring him information."

"So they might be seen as some sort of feathered Irregulars?" I offered, hoping to lighten the mood.

Holmes shot me a reproving look, but then chuckled in spite of himself. "Very good, Watson."

Feeling that things had returned to normal, I observed, "Rather an interesting fellow, that Lasalandra. And I must say for an Italian, his English is nearly flawless."

"It should be," replied Holmes.

"Oh?"

"He was educated at Cambridge."

"You are making that up."

"I may do a great many things, but I do not make things up – unless, of course, a case requires it."

"Then how did you arrive at that conclusion?"

"Had you looked more carefully, you might have noticed that his tie pin was engraved with the Cambridge insignia."

"Come now, Holmes. He could have picked that up anywhere."

"Yes, and I suppose the matching cufflinks were simply another fortuitous find. After all, he is a treasure hunter of sorts." With that he smiled smugly and reaching for his cherrywood pipe, he filled it with shag. After several minutes had passed, he pulled one of his yearbooks down and began to comb through it carefully. Speaking more to himself than me, he asked, "What are we to make of these recent events and our unexpected visitors?"

Since I understood he wasn't expecting an answer, I ventured none. Feeling that Holmes would be happier left to his own devices, I decided to finally organize my notes from one of our recent adventures which I had tentatively titled "The Case of the Vacuous Vintner." This adventure was one that I had not been involved in as it had occurred during that period when I believed my friend had perished at the hands of Professor Moriarty at the Reichenbach Falls in Switzerland.

Holmes had related the details of the case to me one evening as we enjoyed a dry, full-bodied Merlot with our supper. It seems that in 1889, the French government had taken the unprecedented step of legally defining wine as the product of fermented grape juice; the Germans took a similar step a few years later in 1892. Holmes had taken some time from his studies of coal tar derivatives while he was working in a laboratory in Montpellier to assist the *police municipal*. His background in chemistry proved invaluable as he was able to prove that a number of highly regarded vintages were, in fact, counterfeits.

"They were taking recent vintages and putting them in discarded bottles from the various wineries. They were even fairly successful at reproducing the corks and branding them."

"So where did they fall short?" I asked.

"The labels. Paper oxidizes at a steady rate. It will not oxidize in one corner and not in another. However, they had two methods for aging their labels. They would bake some of them in an oven and treat others with various chemicals, including tobacco juice, in an attempt to recreate that aged appearance.

"After examining a number of labels, I realized that in several cases the oxidation was not consistent across the entire label. Child's play, really," I recall him saying.

At that point, I realized Holmes was directly behind me, reading over my shoulder. So engrossed in my work had I been that I hadn't heard him creep up behind me.

"And have you settled on a title for my little chemistry demonstration?" he inquired.

"I am thinking of calling it 'The Case of the Vacuous Vintner.'"

"Why 'vacuous'?" he asked. "I should think 'venal' would be a better adjective." And with that, he turned away, and I heard him mumbling "Vacuus, vacui, vacuo, vacuum, vacuo, vacue."

As he continued his recitation, I said, "I know it's a second declension noun. You are not the only one who had to suffer through the horrors of Latin, you know. *Horror vacui*."

"What did you just say?"

I said "'*Horror vacui*.' The horrors of Latin."

At that Holmes gave me a quizzical look and then he headed for the door.

"I say, what are you up to, old man?"

Rather than answer, Holmes proceeded to grab his hat and stick, "I may not be back in time for dinner," he yelled over his shoulder as he descended the steps.

I went to the window, where I watched him follow his usual procedure, and take the third cab that came along. As his hansom clattered away in the direction of Marylebone Road, I could only ask myself, "What was that all about?"

Chapter 8

I have no idea what time Holmes returned that night. I waited until nearly midnight before retiring, and then I gave up my lonely vigil. There was no sign of him at breakfast the next morning, and as it was nearing the noon hour, I must confess that I was beginning to worry.

At exactly noon, I heard the bell ring, and a few minutes later, Mrs. Hudson ushered an elderly gentleman into our rooms. "I am Simon Turner, and I am looking for Mr. Sherlock Holmes."

Although he was rather stooped, I judged him to be about Holmes' height, and the thick gray beard and muttonchops concealed most of his face. Adding to the disguise was a pair of lightly tinted glasses. Realizing that it was Holmes, I decided to play along.

"Mr. Holmes is not here at the moment. I am his colleague Dr. John Watson, may I be of assistance?"

"I think not, Doctor, unless you can tell me when Mr. Holmes will return. I am a very busy man, and I have several other engagements to which I must attend."

"Did Mr. Holmes say what time he would meet you?"

"He requested that I be here at noon." Pulling a heavy gold pocket watch from his vest, he glanced at it and said, "It is now five minutes past the hour. I shall give him five more minutes and then I must be on my way."

"Would you care for anything? Tea, perhaps, or coffee?"

"I should very much like Mr. Holmes to arrive."

After two more minutes had passed, I began to tire of the game. "Come now, Holmes. I can last as long as you can."

"Excuse me?"

"The jig is up. I recognized you from the moment you entered our rooms." I was just reaching over to grasp the fake beard and pull it off when I heard footsteps dashing up the stairs and then Holmes burst through the door."

All I could think was "Thank goodness Holmes had saved me from myself."

"Ah, Mr. Turner, my sincerest apologies. I know how busy you are, but there was an overturned wagon on Green Street that caused a delay of several minutes."

"Time is money, Mr. Holmes. Now, how may I assist you?"

Pulling his handkerchief from his pocket, Holmes carefully placed it on the table and then unwrapped it. In the middle sat a single clear stone. I thought it might be the diamond that Holmes had discovered in Ralph Prescott's artificial leg.

Pulling a jeweler's loupe from his pocket, Turner turned to Holmes and said, "Have you any tweezers?'

Fetching one from his chemistry table, Holmes handed it to Turner who then screwed the jeweler's loupe into his eye and picked up the stone with the tiny tongs. Taking it to the window, he examined it carefully. When he had finished, he said, "This is a remarkable stone. May I ask how you come to possess it?"

"It actually belongs to a friend," replied Holmes.

Turner looked at Holmes, grunted and returned to examining the diamond. After another minute or two, he handed the stone to Holmes. "I will not bore you with the history of diamond-cutting, but I will tell you that this stone is quite old, and it features what we call a table cut, one of the earliest cuts, dating from the late Middle Ages or early Renaissance. You never see it anymore because it has fallen out of fashion, having given way to such innovations as the Rose cut, Mazarin cut, the Peruzzi cut and the Old European cut. As tools and techniques improved, so too did the cuts – each of those I have just mentioned adds to the number of facets and thus the stone's brilliance."

"So this dates from the medieval period?" I asked.

"Somewhat later, I should say," replied Turner, "perhaps the beginning or the middle of the Renaissance. Without knowing more, such as its country of origin or the type of setting in which it was placed, I would be hard-pressed to date it exactly, but if you insisted upon an answer, I should say the stone dates from around 1300 – give or take a century either way."

Glancing at Holmes, I thought I detected a brief smile play across his face.

"In what type of setting might this diamond have been placed?" asked Holmes.

"It might have been placed in a ring or a brooch or perhaps it adorned an ornate sword hilt or cup. It is impossible to say."

"Thank you, Mr. Turner. You have provided me with some invaluable information."

"Next time, you request my assistance, do try to be punctual, Mr. Holmes." With that he bowed and left our rooms.

"What was that all about?" I asked.

"I was hoping to prove a theory, and Mr. Turner has significantly advanced the narrative I am constructing."

"In what way?"

"Consider, Watson. Prescott was carrying two drawings in his artificial leg – as well as a valuable diamond."

"So that *was* the stone Prescott had concealed in his leg."

"Yes, I managed to prevail upon Lestrade to let me borrow it, so that an expert could examine it. But the question remains: Why would he need a sketch of the Mérode Cup, which is safely ensconced in a museum as well as a real diamond from the early Renaissance?"

"Why indeed?"

"I can conceive of at least three different possible explanations at present."

"Only three?"

"I am certain that more may present themselves as the investigation progresses, but for now, there are three different avenues – all of which warrant further exploration."

I was about to press Holmes for the various explanations when our bell rang. A few moments later, there was a knock on the door.

"Do come in Mrs. Hudson," said Holmes.

With that our landlady entered the room. "This just arrived for you, Mr. Holmes."

Taking a small white envelope from her, Holmes thanked her and then ushered her out of the room. "I believe I recognize Mycroft's scrawl," he said. Opening it, he pulled a small sheet of note paper from inside. After unfolding it, he glanced at it and said, "It seems we have been summoned. Are you free this evening?"

"Certainly, if you need me," I answered.

"Excellent. What say we dine at Simpson's and then walk to the Diogenes afterward? Mycroft has requested our presence at eight."

I was a little low on funds, but before I could say anything, Holmes announced, "It will be my treat."

I have no idea whether Holmes was just in a jubilant mood or whether he had somehow divined my rather precarious financial situation, but I accepted his offer with no further hesitation.

While Holmes opted for the beef at Simpson's, which is always remarkable, I ordered a saddle of lamb with mint sauce and red currant jelly. Holmes also selected a fine Burgundy which complemented our meals perfectly. As we walked to the Diogenes Club, I wondered what need Mycroft might have of his brother's services.

After we arrived and were led into the Stranger's Room, Mycroft joined us a few minutes later. Trailing behind him was a valet, carrying a silver tray with two crystal decanters, three glasses and a gasogene.

After we had exchanged pleasantries, Mycroft lowered his considerable bulk into a wingchair that groaned under his weight. "I wasn't sure whether you would prefer brandy or a single malt after your dinner at Simpson's."

"How could you possibly know where we dined?" I exclaimed.

Mycroft merely smiled and said, "I am certain that my brother can explain."

Holmes chuckled and said, "You have a small stain from the red currant jelly on the outside of your right cuff. I hadn't the heart to tell you and distract you from the lamb that you seemed to be relishing."

I looked at Mycroft and said, "Is that it?"

He nodded and added, "It is a rather distinctive red." Seeing my discomfort, he added, "However, I am certain Mrs. Hudson will be able to get the stain out."

Holmes and I opted for brandy while Mycroft poured himself two fingers of the single malt. "Are you sure I can't persuade you to try this? It's from the Highlands, and it's quite an amazing blend of subtle peat with just a hint of sweetness."

"Some other time, perhaps," Holmes replied. "Since you summoned us, I can only conclude that it must be a matter of some importance."

"How did you enjoy your visit to the South Kensington Museum yesterday?" Mycroft asked nonchalantly.

"Everyone seems to know my business these days," replied my friend rather testily.

"Yes, I had forgotten that you were waylaid by Lestrade at the entrance the previous day. Nothing serious, I hope."

"I am certain that you know exactly why Lestrade was waiting for us. The bigger question is: Are you having me followed?"

At that Mycroft chuckled heartily, "Dear boy, I have far more important assignments for my agents than following you. Rest assured, it was merely a coincidence that one of my men spotted you and Watson there and relayed that information to me."

Holmes appeared to let that sink in, and as Mycroft prepared to sip his whisky, Holmes suddenly asked his brother, "As you know, I don't believe in coincidences, but even if I were so inclined, you also knew about our encounter with Lestrade on the previous day. Two of your men spotting me at the museum on two different days at two different times – I think not, brother mine."

I believe that is the first and only time in my life that I have ever seen Mycroft taken aback – albeit ever so briefly. Rather than answer, he smiled at Sherlock and said, "Touché."

Changing the subject, Mycroft said, "I am certain when you were there, you noticed the area near the entrance had been marked off."

"Yes, I understand that Sir Aston Webb has designed a new building for the museum," replied Holmes.

"So he has. Now what I am about to tell you is a matter that must remain top secret. You are probably not aware of it, but plans are in the works to change the name from the South Kensington Museum to the Victoria and Albert Museum. Should things go as planned that information will become public when Her Majesty lays the foundation stone for the new building. Unfortunately, that will not occur for several years, and hopefully Her Majesty will live long enough to see it."

"What has this to do with me?" said Holmes.

"If what I suspect is going on is indeed happening, you must put a stop to it. There must be no hint of scandal attached to the South Kensington Museum prior to, and hopefully long after its renaming."

"Ah, perhaps you mean the embarrassment of having a prize piece discovered to be counterfeit? Something along those general lines?"

"Something along those exact lines," replied Mycroft. "I have some small say in how the museum allocates its funds, and in the case of extremely costly acquisitions, I have a somewhat larger say."

"I should like a list of everyone who has a say – big or small –in the museum's acquisitions. If you could provide the two lists, I will cross-check them myself."

"Sherlock, I know these people. I would be willing to vouch for them."

"Yes and I am certain that there were people who would have vouched for Jack the Ripper – not knowing who he really was."

"Your point is well taken."

"I will also need a list a list of all the acquisitions that cost the museum in excess of £1,000."

Holmes turned to me and said, "And there you have it. It is incredibly easy to obtain what you need when my brother's interests happen to parallel the Crown's in every way."

Before Mycroft could say anything, Holmes continued with just a hint of sarcasm, "Of course to be fair, it could just be a fortuitous coincidence."

Rather than continue their verbal sparring, Mycroft managed a feeble smile. "Sherlock, I am well aware of the growing market in forgeries. I am simply appealing to you as an Englishman to spare the Queen any embarrassment during her lifetime – and to keep her legacy pristine as well."

I knew that Mycroft had scored a definite touch. Like any Englishman, Holmes was quite fond of Queen Victoria, and I was well aware of his admiration for her – as the wall in our flat attested.

"I shall keep that in mind as I pursue this case."

"That is all I can ask," said Mycroft, "and if you think that I may be of assistance, do not hesitate to call upon me."

After we had left the Diogenes, we decided to walk home since it was a pleasant evening. I kept turning everything I knew over in my mind, but I could make little sense of it. Finally, I turned to my friend. "Holmes, I can see the vague outlines of a case, but I can make neither head nor tail of what we are to do next."

"Not to worry, Watson. While I was out this morning, I made a number of enquiries. I also sent several wires and I am waiting to see what the responses may be. To a large degree, those answers will help us set a course."

"Well, I am certainly glad that things are clearer to you than they are to me."

"What a serendipitous choice of words," he exclaimed, leaving me more confused than I had been previously. "I shall endeavor to make everything as transparent as possible."

"Holmes, you can be most exasperating."

"I am not trying to be opaque by design," he explained. "It is simply that I am still trying to work out certain aspects of this case. But to be fair, I shall pose a question. It is the same one to which I am searching for an answer.

"Why would a man carry an artificial form of glass that harkens to the medieval period as well as a real diamond from the same era? Further, why conceal one but not the other? And why would he hide the diamond and two drawings in an artificial limb?"

"I am sure that I don't know."

"At the moment, I cannot answer all of these questions either although I am developing some theories. However, those considerations pale beside the most confusing aspect of this entire affair."

"Which is?"

"Why did Prescott wish to see us in the first place?"

Chapter 9

Holding firm to his notion that digestion slowed his brain, Holmes eschewed virtually all sustenance when he was consumed by a case. As his friend and physician, I had often advised him that despite his own inclinations to the contrary, sleep and food were necessary. As you might expect, he gave in grudgingly and continued to call them "necessary evils," despite my protestations to the contrary.

It was two days later that I came down to breakfast to find that Holmes had once again gone out early. I spent the morning seeing a few patients and when I returned for lunch, I found my friend sitting at the table and enjoying the repast which Mrs. Hudson had prepared for him.

"You seem in better spirits today," I remarked.

"Yes, it has been a most productive morning. I learned that Mr. Prescott lost his leg in the Anglo-Zulu War. And that the prosthesis was made for him by an artisan in Camberwell who specializes in such devices.

"I have also received the lists from Mycroft," he said holding up two sheets of paper, "of those who have a voice in how the South Kensington Museum spends its money. Fortunately, there are only three names that appear on both lists, if you exclude Mycroft."

"Surely, you don't think someone would try to profit from such a position?"

Holmes looked at me incredulously. "I have known men who would do far worse for far less. Quite frankly, you naiveté surprises me, Watson."

"I wasn't talking so much about the larceny that lurks in the soul of each of us, but of the loss of a reputation and the disgrace that would certainty ensue if one were caught in such an endeavour."

"In the last five years the museum has been on something of a spending spree. They have made hundreds of acquisitions and, believe it or not, there have been several each year that exceeded the £1,000 limit."

"Do you suspect someone of encouraging the museum to purchase counterfeits?"

"I merely state the facts; you may draw your own conclusions."

All of a sudden, I heard the doorbell ring and the sound of muffled voices from below. A few minutes later, Mrs. Hudson knocked on the door.

"Come in Mrs. Hudson," said Holmes.

Our landlady opened the door and poking her head into the room announced, "The Rev. Terrence O'Rourke would like to see you Mr. Holmes. He says it is a matter of some urgency."

"Do show him up, Mrs. Hudson. And perhaps another pot of tea if you would be so kind."

A few minutes later, a large ruddy-faced man entered our rooms. He was dressed all in black, save for the collar that proclaimed him a man of the cloth. He seemed quite agitated and looked at us, shifting his gaze from one to the other.

"I trust you had a pleasant trip from Brighton. I am certain the seaside is lovely this time of year. How are things at

St. John the Baptist? Has it changed much in the past decade? By the way, this is your first visit to London, is it not?"

Father O'Rourke stood there with his mouth agape. When he finally found the words, he said, "What they say about you is true! But how on Earth could you possibly know those things about me?" he continued, appearing totally nonplussed after this exchange.

Having seen similar demonstrations previously, I sat there chuckling at the look of utter amazement on the clergyman's face. Although I had scrutinized the man rather carefully, I knew that as Holmes might have said, "I had seen but he had observed." So like the good priest, I sat waiting for Holmes to explain his wizardry.

"Your tan tells me that you spend a great deal of time outdoors. No one in London has the deep tan and ruddy complexion that you possess, Father."

"That may be true, but I might have come from Torquay or Devon. How did you deduce Brighton?"

"The top of your return ticket is just jutting out of your breast pocket."

"And so it is," said the priest, delightedly pulling it out for me to examine. "And I suppose, you guessed at the church and got lucky."

Holmes shot me a pained expression. Turning to the priest, he replied, "I never guess. Your watch fob is a gold St. John the Baptist medal that reads 1835-1885. That leads me to think you that you have been there longer than nine years to warrant such a display of affection from your parishioners. As for your first trip to London – that was the easiest of all.

"Despite the train ride and the cab ride, your garments look as though they were freshly ironed. That tells me that all your attire is new; add to that shoes that positively gleam and a stiff new collar – no one gets that dressed up to see a detective. However, they might if they were planning on taking in some sights – perhaps Westminster Abbey as sort of a clergyman's holiday."

"Everything you say is true, Mr. Holmes, so I am hoping that you can help me."

"I make no promises, Father, as I have several cases at hand at the moment, but do tell me the particulars."

"Although we are the oldest parish in Brighton, we are by no means wealthy. So when we were robbed recently, we informed the police, but they have been able to shed no light on the matter."

"Robbed? Pray tell, what was taken?"

"Two gold chalices and two patens."

"Anything else?"

"No, and that's the strangest part, Mr. Holmes. There were several valuable icons in the church as well as money in the poor boxes, but the two chalices and patens were the only things taken."

"Is there anything remarkable about either the chalices or the patens?"

"Just their age. One was perhaps forty years old and the other twenty. They were left to the church by two priests who had served there and passed away."

"Were there other chalices in the church?"

"There were two others – mine and Monsignor Darcy's."

"Were they all kept together?"

"No. Our two chalices were locked in cases in the vestry while the others were kept on side altars in the church."

"And when did this occur?"

"Perhaps two weeks ago, give or take a few days."

"Well, I wish I could be of more help Father, but it sounds as though it were a simple crime of opportunity. Some poor soul gave into temptation and couldn't resist, what's the phrase you Catholics use? A 'near occasion of sin'?

"At any rate, I am certain the trail has gone cold by now, and whatever clues might have been present have been ground underfoot – both by your parishioners and the police."

"I thought you might say that, Mr. Holmes, and if those were the circumstances, I should never have bothered you."

"Oh, is there more to the story?" inquired Holmes.

"As it happens, there is. When you mentioned a clergyman's holiday, you weren't far off. The Rev. Jack Griffin, with whom I attended the seminary, is to be named the new pastor of St Etheldreda's R C Church on Ely Street in Holborn. He and I have been friends for more than twenty years, and he invited me to attend his installation.

"During our correspondence, I told him about the robbery at St. John the Baptist, and he informed me that St. Etheldreda's had recently suffered a similar misfortune."

"What was taken and when?" asked Holmes eagerly.

"In his letter, he wrote a chalice, a paten and two gold candlesticks had been stolen," replied the priest. "Although I received the letter only yesterday, he said the theft had occurred some three weeks ago."

"Do you happen to know if he reported the theft to the papers?"

"Indeed, he did. In fact, he sent me the article from *The Times*." The priest then reached into his breast pocket and extracted a folded piece of newspaper, which he handed to Holmes.

"I see that the pieces were also made of gold," remarked my friend.

"That would not be unusual," replied the priest, "Most items that appear on the altar are usually made of gold although some are also constructed of silver."

"Father, you have my word that I will look into these thefts, but I am not optimistic," said Holmes.

"Thank you, Mr. Holmes. I will be staying at St. Etheldreda's until Monday next should you care to reach me."

"I shouldn't be at all surprised if we meet again," said Holmes. "I should very much like to speak to Father Griffin. In fact, why don't you arrange that and let me know when the good Father is free."

"You have my word, Mr. Holmes. Thank you and God bless," said the priest as he departed.

After I had heard the front door close, I turned to Holmes, who was sitting at the table writing and said, "What do you make of that?"

"I find it interesting, confusing and enlightening – all at the same time," he replied.

"I certainly agree that it is interesting and confusing – I am not so certain it was all that illuminating."

"Come, Watson. The connection is so obvious a child could see it."

"Not this child," I huffed. And then I quickly added, "Connection to what?"

With that, Holmes finished his writing, strode to the window, opened it and yelled to the street below, "Find Wiggins and tell him I should like to see him at once."

I heard the voice of a boy yell back, "Righto, guv."

He then pulled one of his indices from the shelf, and after turning the pages furiously for a minute, began jotting down notes. I knew better than to interrupt him when he had picked up a scent, so I contented myself with the morning papers.

Perhaps fifteen minutes later, I heard the bell ring and shortly after that, I heard the clatter of footsteps as a pair of young legs bolted up the stairs, followed by a knock on the door.

"Come in, Wiggins." yelled Holmes.

A young street urchin, perhaps fifteen, entered our rooms. "You wanted to see me, Mr. 'Olmes."

"I have a task for you and the rest of the Irregulars," my friend said.

The boy's face lit up. After straightening himself up and removing his cap, Wiggins bowed to Holmes and without the least trace of an accent, he said, "We are at your service, Mr. Holmes."

He then looked at me, smiled mischievously and said, "'Ow's that Doctor? I been practicing me proper English."

I refrained from laughing but I did see a smile cross Holmes' face. "That's excellent, Wiggins. The more you can do, the more opportunities will present themselves to you."

The grin on the boy's face broadened so that you would have thought Holmes had just knighted the lad.

All of a sudden, there was another knock on the door. "Do come in, Mrs. Hudson," said Holmes.

Our landlady entered and she looked at me, "Dr. Watson, do you think you might assist me in the kitchen for a moment."

Although I desperately wanted to hear Holmes' instructions to Wiggins, I could not refuse her request. When I returned a few minutes later, Wiggins was gone. Holmes looked at me and said, "I trust you were able to remedy the clogged drain for her."

"I'm not even going to ask."

"No great stretch of deduction required, Doctor. When you left your sleeves were crisp and the creases sharp; now they are winkled as though you had rolled them up to avoid getting them wet.

"Besides, I had to address a similar situation for her two days ago, and I suggested that if it should happen again, you were eminently more qualified than I to deal with such a matter – having owned a house yourself."

Hearing that I sighed and cautioned my friend, "Holmes, just remember that every dog has its day."

"That may well be, but if you are not busy, would you care to assist me?"

"By all means. What do you have in mind?"

"I'm going to step around to St. Cyprian's at Clarence Gate. If you would pay a visit to St. Marylebone, I should be most appreciative."

"And what exactly am I looking for?"

"Just ask one of the priests if anything has gone missing within the past few weeks. I shall do the same, and we can meet back here in an hour and compare notes?"

"As you wish."

Holmes had much the shorter walk to St. Cyprian's but as the day was sunny and warm, I was thoroughly enjoying my stroll through the neighborhood.

Having tended to several members of the congregation, as well as one of the priests, I was somewhat familiar with the church and its history. I knew Byron had been baptized there and that the Brownings had wed there. Upon arriving and introducing myself, I was led into the office of the Rev. Paul Beichner.

"Doctor Watson, I am pleased to meet you. You will pardon me if I ask: Are you *the* Doctor Watson?"

I admitted that I was and then he professed, "I do so enjoy your stories in The Strand each month." And then it hit him, "Are you here on a case?"

"Perhaps," I replied, "Mr. Holmes is investigating thefts from several churches, and he wanted to inquire whether any items of value might have gone missing."

Strange as it may sound, he seemed deeply disappointed when he said, "As far as I know, everything is accounted for."

"Chalices?" I asked, prodding him.

"We keep them under lock and key in the vestry," he advised me."

"Candlesticks?"

"Again, all accounted for."

"Well, if something should go missing, please contact either Mister Holmes or myself." I handed the priest one of my cards.

"Indeed, I will," said the priest. Then we shook hands, he thanked me, and I headed back to Baker Street. I was in rather a hurry as I wanted to press Holmes about what exactly he had asked Wiggins to carry out, but when I returned, the flat was empty.

On the table, I spotted an envelope bearing the initials "J.W." in my friend's rather distinctive hand. Upon opening it, I extracted a single piece of paper.

> *Watson,*
> *Nothing missing from St. Cyprian's. I had*
> *to step out rather unexpectedly. I hope to*
> *be back in time for dinner, but you know*
> *how these things go.*
>
> *S.H.*

I was all too familiar with how "these things go," so I wasn't anticipating a timely return from my friend; as a result, I was not overly disappointed when he did not appear for our evening meal. When she arrived to remove the dishes, Mrs. Hudson said, "I'll make him a plate and he can fetch it from the kitchen if he returns home hungry."

I was torn. On the one hand, I desperately wanted to learn about the summons that had demanded my friend's attention, but at the same time, I was somewhat put out that he had rather unceremoniously left me behind. I considered going to my club, but in the end, I remained home reading until close to midnight when I decided to turn in.

When I came down for breakfast the next morning, Holmes was sitting at the table drinking coffee and reading *The Times.* Before I could say anything, he started the conversation by saying, "I trust you didn't wait up for me too late."

"Not at all," I lied. Feigning nonchalance, I countered with, "I trust you had a productive evening."

"I would say so, yes," he replied, and then he resumed reading the papers.

Holmes can be maddening at times, and this was proving to be one of those occasions. Deciding two could play at that game, I picked up a copy of *The Daily Telegraph.* The silence continued for several moments and when I finally peered over my paper, I saw Holmes grinning at me.

"Dash it all," I said.

"I was wondering how long you could hold out. I must say I am impressed. Now I suppose I owe you an explanation and then I will be happy to answer any questions you might pose."

Despite myself, I couldn't help chuckling. "We have been at this a long time, haven't we?"

"I had dispatched Wiggins and the Irregulars to various pawn shops to see if anyone had recently tried to secure a loan for gold candlesticks. I also instructed them to be on the lookout for any chalices or patens. As I expected, their efforts proved fruitless."

"If you thought they would return empty-handed, why send them on a fool's errand?"

"It was hardly that, Watson. I was eliminating one possibility so that I might focus my attention on what I believe to be the crux of this mystery. Consider, a person normally steals something because he or she desires it or sees an opportunity to convert it to ready cash. Given the fact, that none of the pieces has been offered up – even at the most disreputable moneylenders – I am inclined to think they were purloined for another purpose entirely."

"And what might that be?"

"I should think that would be fairly obvious, but if it hasn't hit you yet, keep working on it. In due time, my friend, I am certain that you will arrive at the same conclusion as I. The path we are following is a most circuitous one, and I need you to focus on the matters at hand rather than the many distractions along the way. After all, this is shaping up as one of my more *outre* cases.

"For the moment though, if you are interested, I need to see a scientist. Would you care to accompany me?"

"I should be delighted." And so it was that a few minutes later, Holmes and I were in a hansom headed for Lambeth. After crossing the Thames, we followed the Albert Embankment to Black Prince Road to Old Paradise Street where we stopped in front of what looked to be a small factory. The sign outside said only "Glassworks."

After we had alighted from the cab, Holmes instructed the driver to wait for us. He then turned and headed for the factory.

"I thought you said you were going to see a scientist."

"And so I am," he replied.

He then entered the front door, and as he did a bell tinkled gently, announcing our presence.

A few minutes later, a young woman entered from the workroom in the rear.

"Dr. Jennifer Wojno?"

"I am," she replied rather nervously. "And might I ask who you are?"

"My name is Sherlock Holmes, and this is my associate, Dr. John Watson."

Surprisingly, she did not react to Holmes' introduction. Truth be told, I don't think she had any idea who he was.

"I have it on good authority that you are one of the foremost authorities on glass in the world today. From what I understand, you are applying the principles of physics to create new and different varieties of glass."

She looked at Holmes curiously. "I do not publicize my work except perhaps in some of the more esoteric scientific journals."

"So I am given to understand. I believe you have created a type of protective glass that is a significant improvement over what is available right now."

"I am still perfecting the process," she said, "but it involves reinforcing the glass with very thin, almost invisible, strands of wire which are actually encased in the glass."

"And I also understand that you are creating new and improved lenses for telescopes."

"You seem very well informed about my affairs, Mr. Holmes. Are you a scientist, yourself?"

"An amateur one at best," he said in a rare display of humility, "but I have acquired a broad range of knowledge on various topics."

"That still doesn't explain how you came to know of me or why you are here."

"I was made aware of your experiments by a friend who works for the government. I don't think I need say more."

"Not at all. How can I help you?" she asked.

"Are you familiar with the term *plique à jour*?" Holmes asked innocently.

However, her reaction told us all we needed to know. Walking to the door, she looked out through the windows. "Is that your cab?" she asked.

"It is," I replied.

She then locked the door. "Since you seem to know so much, I might as well tell you everything. A few years ago, when

I was first getting started, I was looking for backers. I met with bankers, financiers, industrialists – to no avail.

"Finally, I was approached by two men – John Roberts and Chester Boles. Mr. Boles, I know, was a jeweler, and they said they would be willing to finance my endeavours if I would be willing to do some work for them in return."

"And you agreed?"

She nodded her head. "This place is my dream. They rented it for me, improved the furnace and provided the materials."

"And in return, you had to produce pieces of *plique à jour* and other things from time to time?"

"Exactly. The first request was only about six months ago. Since that time, they would visit once a month or so to give me directions, and then someone would visit a few days later to pick up the finished pieces."

"And that was the extent of it?"

"Not entirely. From time to time, Mr. Boles would bring me gold pieces to melt down and molds for the molten metal."

"Was it always gold?"

"Yes, sir."

"I don't suppose any of the molds are still here?"

"No, sir. Mr. Boles would come and bring the gold and the molds and take them away when I had finished."

"Do you remember exactly what you created?"

"He had a mold for a small beaker or cup with a matching top."

"Sort of like the Mérode Cup?" I interjected.

"I don't know what that is," she replied.

"What else did you make?" asked Holmes, seizing control of the conversation.

"There were these button-like things, and there were also platters or plates."

"And when was the last time you saw either Boles or Roberts?" asked Holmes.

"I saw Mr. Boles about three weeks ago. At that time, he had me make several of those button-like things and a plate."

"And Mr. Roberts?"

"I haven't seen him for at least two or three months," she replied, "perhaps longer."

"I will not trouble you any longer," said Holmes. "However, may I call upon you again, should the need arise?"

"By all means," she replied.

After we had exited the shop, I said, "So, what are you thinking?"

"I believe her, Watson. You could sense her enthusiasm for science, and I think she unknowingly entered into an agreement with the two blackguards."

As we climbed into the cab, Holmes stopped and reaching in, extracted an envelope. "What's this?"

Speaking to the cabby, Holmes said, "Did you see the person who left this?"

"I didn't see anyone," he replied.

"Did you speak to anyone?"

"Just some bloke who needed directions."

Holmes smiled, gave the driver an address in Pall Mall and climbed into the hansom. I entered and sat opposite him.

"What does it say?" I asked.

Extracting a penknife from his pocket, Holmes slit the envelope and withdrew a single sheet of paper. He read it once and chuckled, and after he had examined it for a few minutes, he handed it to me.

I gazed at it. In the middle of the page was a single line:

"Dear me, Mr. Holmes! Dear me!"

Chapter 10

"Holmes," I exclaimed, "that sounds a great deal like the missive you received following the death of Birdy Edwards."

"To the letter, Watson. I am afraid that this is becoming far more treacherous than even I had imagined."

"But Moriarty is dead, and Sebastian Moran is in prison."

"Do you remember recently when you chided me for declining *vacuus*? And you uttered the phrase '*Horror vacui*'?"

"Of course, you wanted me to change 'vacuous' to 'venal' in the title of that adventure, and I was lamenting the horrors of learning Latin."

"Exactly! However, you need to brush up on your linguistic skills, old friend. Translated literally '*horror vacui*' would be 'horrible void,' but the more popular translation is taken from Aristotle's time-honored idiom: Nature abhors a vacuum."

"You don't mean…"

"I am afraid that is it exactly. With no Moriarty and no Moran, there is a vacuum in the criminal underworld, and just as I am sure that you are sitting opposite me, that's how certain I am that someone has stepped in to fill that void."

The rest of the journey back to our rooms was spent in silence. To say I was taken aback by Holmes' revelation would be an understatement. However, the more I thought about it, the more sense it made.

When we had reached our home and Holmes had settled in his chair with his briar and his shag, I broached the subject. "Could the heir apparent be this Roberts fellow who accompanied Boles to the glassmaker's and was spotted at the jeweler's store?"

"I am inclined to doubt it. This plan to create counterfeit artifacts requires a great deal of thought and planning. It also needs willing bodies to execute – perhaps a poor choice of words there – certain commands.

"No, Watson, I do not think this new criminal overlord would be caught carrying out his own dirty work. You remember how hard I had to work to build a case against Moriarty?"

"Indeed, I do."

"I hardly think this new acolyte, if he has learned anything from his master, would involve himself so directly with anything of so sordid a nature."

"So we have no idea for whom we are searching then?"

"No, Watson, but we do know several things about our quarry. He is well-educated and cultured to have devised a scheme this nefarious. He is well-to-do, and he is also quite brutal."

"Why you might be describing Moriarty himself!"

"We also have a few leads that we can follow – the most promising being this Roberts fellow. My guess is that he is nothing more than a pilot fish, but if we can apprehend him, perhaps he will lead us to the shark at the top of the food chain."

"That's certainly a lead worth pursuing. But how can you locate one man in all of London?"

"We will start by assigning a contingent of Irregulars to monitor Dr. Wojno's workshop. We have no guarantee Roberts will return, but I will arrange it so that if he does, the Irregulars will know immediately and I will know shortly thereafter.

"There are other steps that we can take as well," Holmes said, and he then proceeded to outline several of them for me.

When he had finished, he said, "We also possess one big advantage. By sending that letter, he has announced himself. So we will hunt him, old friend, just as Colonel Moran hunted tigers – silently, without giving anything away – and when he walks beneath our blind, we will have him."

I said, "It certainly seems as though you have been giving this some serious thought."

Holmes merely smiled and filled his pipe. A few moments later, I could see that he was deep in thought. When supper arrived, Holmes barely touched his food, even though the steak and kidney pie that Mrs. Hudson had prepared was quite tasty.

After dinner he returned to his chair and fired up the briar. I knew this was going to be what Holmes referred to as a "three-pipe problem," so I contented myself with reading and catching up on my correspondence until after ten. Holmes was still a study in concentration, so I bade him goodnight and headed off to bed.

When I awoke the next morning, I fully expected to find him sitting in his chair, knees drawn up, fingers steepled, much as I had left him the previous evening. As a result, I was pleasantly surprised, and puzzled, to learn from Mrs. Hudson that he had departed about two hours earlier.

When he returned shortly after noon, he was excited, but I decided to let him tell me what had transpired in his own time.

After asking Mrs. Hudson for a pot of coffee, he looked at me and said, "I suppose you would like to know what I have been up to."

"Only if you feel like sharing, old man."

"I began by arranging for the Irregulars to keep watch on Dr. Wojno's shop. I spoke with her, and if Roberts should visit, she will escort him to his cab, wipe her forehead with her sleeve and bid him a good day. That will be the signal for the Irregulars to follow him.

"I also had her create something for me that I feel will be of interest to whomever is responsible for creating these frauds.

"After that I visited Mycroft, and he has arranged a small private gathering at the museum tomorrow night in order to discuss the next possible acquisition. I have arranged for the two of us to be invited. Do bring your cheque book, Watson. It is a fundraiser after all."

"And what is it that the museum will be seeking to acquire."

"Mycroft asked the same question, and truth be told, I think the answer will depend upon whatever Madame Pittorino suggests. I plan to visit her shortly. Are you free?"

"Sadly, no. I am covering for a colleague, but you will tell me all about it?"

"Of course," he replied. After downing a cup of coffee, he was out the door, and I didn't see him again until that evening.

"How did it go?" I asked when he finally arrived home sometime after seven.

"Splendidly," he replied. "Madame Pittorino has suggested that we let it be known that the Founder's Jewel might be available. That's something the museum could hardly pass up an opportunity to secure."

"Founder's Jewel?"

"You've never heard of it?"

"Can't say that I have," I replied.

"It's a brooch, old man."

"And what makes it so special?"

"To begin with it is constructed in the shape of an M. The arches appear to resemble Gothic windows. Standing in the windows are figures of the Virgin Mary and Gabriel, the angel of the Annunciation. The entire scene is surmounted by a crown. As you might expect, it is bejeweled and it is stunning."

"Where is it now? Does Madame Pittorino have it?"

Holmes laughed, "No, Watson. It resides at New College at Oxford. It was bequeathed to the institution by William of Wykeham in 1404.

"However, with a little help from Mycroft, the Founder's Jewel just may appear to become available at auction. Now, if you will excuse me, I have a few more tasks to which I must attend. Remember, the gala is at 8 o'clock tomorrow night – formal dress." With that, Holmes let himself out and I did not see nor hear from him again until the following evening at dinner time."

Just as I was preparing to eat, Mrs. Hudson knocked on the door. "I have a note from Mr. Holmes," she said.

Taking it from her, I pulled a single sheet of paper from the envelope.

"Watson,
I have been unavoidably delayed. I shall meet you at the
reception. Don't forget your cheque book.
S.H.

With no other options, I dressed, and at half seven, I descended the stairs and hailed a cab to take me to the museum.

After alighting from the cab, I made my way into the main lobby, which had been decorated with little niches – each of which contained one of the museum's many treasures. They were separated by flowing curtains that hung from the ceiling. They gave the artifacts a sort of intimate viewing space that reminded me a bit of the confessionals that I had seen in the few Roman Catholic churches I had visited.

All told, there were perhaps fifty people there, and while I recognized a few faces from their photographs in the newspaper, I don't believe I actually knew anyone there, except for Holmes, of course.

That all changed shortly when I saw Mycroft enter, which I must admit took me by surprise, as I had never known him to venture far from the Diogenes Club or his office in Whitehall. A few minutes later Mr. Burkhardt joined the soiree.

Burkhardt also spotted me and shortly thereafter, he joined me. "Mr. Holmes is not with you?"

"No, he has been delayed, but I am expecting him."

"I had hoped to speak with him. When you see him, please give him that message for me?"

"I certainly will, but aren't you a bit out of your element here?"

"Not at all," he laughed. "The museums are not rivals – except on those occasions when we both seek to acquire the same item. As you might expect, I need to keep an eye on the competition." With that, he excused himself and began exchanging pleasantries with an older couple.

Waiters were passing canapés and glasses of wine, but I wanted a clear head, so after my first glass, I refrained from any further indulgence.

A few minutes later, a small bell tinkled, and Sir Edward Hargreaves, the director of the museum, introduced himself. He explained that if the rumors were true, an extremely rare artifact was about to become available, and the museum had every intention of acquiring it. His remarks generated a polite smattering of applause. He then said, he was going to have the members of the Acquisitions Committee say a few words and he began by introducing Lord Charles Danvers. He in turn welcomed everyone again and then proceeded to prattle on interminably about the mission of the museum. He concluded by reiterating Hargreaves' words and encouraging everyone to give generously to this new campaign. "This is one we don't want to let get away," he concluded.

After Danvers had finished, Lord James Howe took his place at the podium and informed the audience that the piece that they anticipated coming to auction in the near future was unique and breathtakingly beautiful. "I dare not say more, lest I ruin the surprise, but like my predecessors here on stage, I would ask all of you to consider making a donation to the museum so that we might secure this piece for visitors to the museum to enjoy."

The speech continued for several more minutes, and I was beginning to wish I had never come. "It will be over soon, old man," said Holmes, who had suddenly materialized at my elbow.

"What the devil! Where have you been?" I whispered.

"Not now, Watson," and with that he turned to pay attention to the next speaker. I was rather surprised to see a striking woman take the podium. "I am Lady Ashley Cox," she said. "Many of you probably knew my late husband, Louis, who served as the director of this museum for more than a decade before his untimely death. When he passed away two years ago,

I was honored to be asked to serve out his term, and now I am just starting my own first term as a member of the committee." Looking closely, I realized that she was not so young as she had first appeared; nonetheless, she was what can only be described as a handsome woman.

She proceeded to reinforce the previous pleas for generosity, and encouraged all those present to think of a gift to the museum as their legacy. "Wouldn't it be wonderful to have your grandchildren visit a gallery bearing your name or your family's name?"

Her speech was mercifully short, and some ten minutes later, Holmes and I were once again in a hansom wending through the city toward Baker Street.

"That was a rather pointless evening," I remarked. In the darkness of the cab, it was impossible to discern Holmes' face and when he failed to respond, I lapsed into a complementary silence. It was only when we were settled in our chairs, brandy poured and pipes lit that Holmes remarked, "I couldn't disagree more."

"Disagree with what?" I replied, having forgotten my earlier remark.

"Your statement in the cab where you described tonight as 'pointless.' I actually found it rather interesting."

"Do tell," I encouraged.

"Such evenings often include a sort of grand gesture by one of the speakers, in which he or she pledges a considerable amount toward the project, to get things rolling as it were. Yet, we saw none of that tonight.

"Still, given the rather precarious financial situations of all three speakers, I am not in the least surprised."

"You can't be serious. How did you come by this information?"

"Lord Danvers recently sold a painting by Hans Holbein, the Younger which has been in his family for generations. As he has only himself to support, one would be hard-pressed to conclude anything else but that he is in dire straits. Also, were he not desperate for cash, I am certain he would have bequeathed the painting to the museum.

"Lord Howe has recently reduced his household staff by half. Moreover, just last month he sold his carriage and replaced it with a much smaller brougham. Hardly the actions of a man enjoying robust financial health."

"You do make a compelling case," I replied, "and Lady Cox?"

"She appears to have been laboring mightily to stave off her husband's creditors and thus far she seems to have been successful. By the way, did you notice her attire?"

"Some sort of emerald green dress," I replied.

"Indeed, but it was the latest design from one of the leading Haute Couture houses in Paris. I'm not sure how you keep the creditors at bay while purchasing a gown such as that. Moreover, had you looked more closely, you would have observed that the only jewelry she wore was a wedding ring, but it was bedecked with diamonds."

"Perhaps she has a benefactor or a new romantic interest," I offered. "After all, Holmes, although you may know little of it, women will not be denied their baubles. You may trust me on that account."

Holmes merely smiled indulgently and then continued as if I had not spoken. "Taken together, these facts and observations prove nothing, and it is proof that we require. Still, they do offer a glimpse into the lives of people pretending to be something other than they are."

"Speaking of such anomalies, might I ask where you spent the evening?"

"I spent the evening serving wine and passing out hors d'oeuvres before I joined you."

"You were there? The entire time?"

"Indeed, and I must say, I admire your restraint. You made it through the entire night with but a single glass of burgundy."

"And did you learn anything of import?"

"Some of what I just related to you was gleaned from servants tonight. The rest of the information I gathered while looking into the backgrounds of the other board members who have a say in the decision-making process. As you might expect, they generally follow Mycroft's lead in such matters – but not always."

I was about to ask him to elaborate when I heard the bell ring. "Who can that be at this late hour?"

Eyes sparkling, Holmes looked at me and said, "Perhaps a new client or perhaps someone who can shed light on this case."

A moment later, Mrs. Hudson tapped on the door. "Come in, Mrs. Hudson," said Holmes.

Our landlady entered and said, "This telegram just arrived for you, Mr. Holmes."

After thanking our landlady, Holmes ripped open the envelope. He perused it carefully and as he did, his face reddened ever so slightly.

Unable to restrain myself any longer, I asked, "What does it say, Holmes?"

He handed it to me: It was a single line of text that read:

"Another glass of champagne, if you please, Mr. Holmes."

Chapter 11

"He mocks me, Watson."

"I am certain you will have the last laugh," I replied.

"Even Moriarty was never so bold," continued Holmes, as though he had not heard me.

"What's to be done?"

"We continue on our present course, but we proceed with a new awareness that our every move is probably being watched. I can only hope that the hubris of this new nemesis may prove instrumental in his undoing."

Holmes continued, "It's late, Watson. Go to bed. Something tells me that we shall be quite busy in the days ahead, and sleep may prove hard to come by."

With that he pulled down one of his reference books, filled his pipe and began turning the pages, slowly and methodically.

As I lay in bed, I thought about the brazenness of this new criminal, and I reflected back on some of the cases Holmes and I had worked on together. Truth be told, aside from Moriarty, I could never recall any criminal with the effrontery to tweak my friend in such a bold manner. "Times are changing," I thought, "and not for the better." Although it took quite a while, I eventually drifted off into a fitful sleep while thoughts of past villains kept running through my head.

I awoke the next morning and after dressing, I went downstairs to find Holmes perusing the papers while drinking coffee. Looking at me, he smiled and said, "It's just after nine. You will certainly catch no worm."

"You seem very chipper this morning," I replied. "Have you received some positive news?"

Leaning forward, he picked up several papers from the table. "I have secured appointments with Lord Danvers at 11, Lord Howe at 1 and Lady Cox at 4. All told, I think that may be considered good news."

"And under what pretext are you meeting these people?"

Holmes smiled placidly and said, "No ruse was necessary. I merely informed them that I was investigating a ring of counterfeiters and asked for their assistance. So since there is no subterfuge involved, you may accompany me as yourself, if you wish."

At exactly 9:45, we descended the stairs and Holmes hailed a hansom. He threw himself into a corner, sank his chin into his chest and said nothing until we had arrived at the Office of the Parliamentary Counsel. We found our way to Lord Danvers' office and were soon ushered inside. Considering his rather lofty position within the government, his office was a Spartan affair – more suited for a military man than a politician – and I wondered if his declining finances had forced him to part with some of his prized possessions.

There were few adornments on the walls and but a single bookcase, filled with various volumes. "Would you gentlemen care for coffee?" Danvers asked. I was surprised when Holmes said yes, as he had just finished two cups earlier. "Just let me tell my secretary," Danvers said.

In the minute or two that he was gone, Holmes prowled the office, glancing at the photos and proclamations on the wall and paying particular attention to the books on Danvers' shelves.

When he rejoined us a moment later, he began by asking, "Now Mr. Holmes, how may I be of service?" Although he was a slight man, he possessed a big, booming voice that belied his stature and a genial disposition. Without going into great detail, Holmes explained that he had been investigating a ring of criminals which specialized in creating bogus artifacts and then selling them to museums and private collectors.

"I rather wondered why you were here," said Danvers, "and now I know. I suppose this has to do with the possible acquisition of the Founder's Jewel for the museum."

"To some degree," replied Holmes.

"We do employ experts to make certain that anything we acquire is genuine, you know," he said.

"I am well aware of that fact," replied my friend, "but sometimes even the most talented expert can fall victim to a clever forgery."

At that point the coffee arrived, and after we had been served, Danvers picked up right where the conversation had left off. "I rather doubt that, Mr. Holmes. Have you detected any forgeries in the museum?" After a pause, he continued, "I thought not. Sir, I serve on the board as a civic duty and because it allows me to satisfy my artistic side. As for acquisitions, I tend to leave such decisions to others who are far more knowledgeable about such things than I."

After a few more questions, Holmes pulled out his watch and the fob came loose and fell to the floor. When Danvers picked it up, he handed it to Holmes and said, "I hope it isn't broken."

"It's just a trinket I found in a pawnshop," he replied. He then thanked Danvers for his time, and we bid him good day and departed. Once we were outside, I looked at Holmes expectantly.

"He's either an exceptionally talented liar, which is certainly a possibility, or he really knows very little about such *objets d'art*. It remains to be seen which is true," said my friend. "Although I must say his taste in books is rather eclectic."

Although it was a fine day and we could have walked to The Royal Exchange, Holmes opted to take a cab. "Perhaps if we arrive just a bit early, we might catch Lord Howe a little off guard." I rather doubted the wisdom of Holmes' remark, but I had to admit there was something to be said for the element of surprise.

At exactly, 12:30, Holmes handed his card to Lord Howe's secretary and explained, "We have a one o'clock appointment, but as our earlier business finished ahead of schedule, we decided to come here directly on the off-chance that Lord Howe might be free."

The young man said nothing but simply nodded and after knocking on an ornate oak door vanished inside Lord Howe's office. A minute later the door was thrown open and Lord Howe came out to greet us. After introductions had been made, he ushered us into his office.

Lavishly decorated, the spacious room stood in stark contrast to that of Lord Danvers. The walls were filled with paintings and photographs, and several bookcases contained not only bound volumes but trophies and mementos that Lord Howe had collected during his travels. I was trying to take everything in as we were urged to sit in two comfortable chairs.

As he settled himself behind an ornate cherrywood desk, I looked at Howe. He was a big man, with a thick mane of silver hair and an impeccably groomed beard and moustache. "I cannot tell you what a pleasure it is to finally meet you." Looking at me, he continued, "I do look forward to your stories in The Strand each month." Turning to Holmes, he added, "I must say the Countess of Morcar is still singing your praises every time I meet her."

Holmes waved the compliment away. "A mere trifle," he said modestly.

Reaching into his desk, Howe pulled out a bottle of Glenmorangie. "I know it's a bit early in the day, but can I interest either of you in a drink?" When we both declined, Howe offered coffee and tea, and we both opted for the latter. Howe then passed the request to his secretary.

While we were waiting, Holmes once again prowled the office, examining the various mementos and the bound volumes. At one point, he muttered something under his breath.

When Howe returned with the coffee, he asked, "What brings you to my office?" Before anyone could answer, he continued, "If you don't mind. I'm going to try my hand at this detective game and assume since I saw you both at the gala, it has something to do with the museum."

Holmes then reiterated the story about the ring of counterfeiters, and how he was hoping to preclude the museum from any possible embarrassment should it, through no fault of anyone, end up securing a bogus artifact.

"Well, as I am sure you know, each item is carefully vetted before we even consider attempting to acquire it."

"True, true," said Holmes, "and I am certain that you are aware that museums around the globe have been duped and ended up purchasing articles for significant sums that turned out to be next to worthless."

"I will admit that we may have made a few injudicious choices in the past," Howe admitted. "However even Pitt-Rivers has been deceived by several clever forgeries."

"That is true," replied Holmes, "but should the museum ever be renamed …" and he left the sentence unfinished.

"Your point is well-taken, Mr. Holmes. I shall exercise an even greater degree of circumspection going forward."

"That is all we can ask," said Holmes. "Just out of curiosity, how did you come by your expertise?"

"While I cannot boast of any formal training," replied Howe, "I have traveled widely and become something of a collector over the years." At that, he gestured to the items on the shelves in his office. "As you might suspect, I have been swindled more than once, and I pride myself on discerning the integrity of the other parties involved. I proudly display my purchases, and I shall leave everything to the museum."

As he spoke, Holmes wandered over to examine a dull red terracotta mask that stood on one of the shelves. "This is stunning," he remarked. "Etruscan, is it not?"

"It is, indeed. I picked that up at an antique store in Athens. I don't believe the owner had any idea of its worth. And I must admit, it is one of the crown jewels in my collection."

"It is one of the finest examples of *bucchero* I have ever seen."

"It is a rather remarkable piece, is it not?" replied Howe.

"Indeed," said Holmes, replacing it carefully. "Thank you for allowing me to examine it."

As Holmes pulled out his watch, the fob once again came loose. Lord Howe picked it and handed it to my friend. "That's a rather unusual fob," he observed.

"Yes," he replied. "I came across it in a pawn shop and was struck by the color."

Glancing at the timepiece, he said to Howe, "Now, I don't want to take up anymore of your time, so let me thank you for your hospitality, and I am certain we shall meet again."

When we had left the building, I could see that Holmes was in a state. Imitating Howe's deep bass, he proclaimed, "I pride myself on discerning the integrity of the other parties involved.

"The man is a fraud, a charlatan, an imposter, Watson. That terracotta mask which I inquired about..."

"Yes, what was the term, you used?"

"*Bucchero*. It was a type of pottery produced by the Etruscans, but it is always dark grey or black – never red."

"So Lord Howe is not the expert he would have us believe?"

"I wouldn't go that far just yet, Watson. He does seem to possess a certain superficial knowledge, but as the poet once opined:

'A little learning is a dangerous thing.' "

We then hailed a cab and Holmes gave the driver an address in St. John's Wood. Some thirty minutes later, we arrived in front of an elegant townhouse, the residence of Lady Ashley Cox.

A servant in full livery answered the bell and showed us into an attractive sitting room with a view of Regent's Park across the street.

Gazing about at the leather-bound volumes that filled the inset bookshelves and the oils that hung on the walls, I looked at Holmes and remarked, "What a difference a mile makes, old man. A bit posher than our digs."

Holmes, who had been busily examining the books that graced the shelves, and grunting occasionally, shot me a reproving glance, for at that moment, the door opened and in walked Lady Ashley Cox. I believe that I had described her as a "handsome woman" earlier, but up close, that description does not even begin to do her justice. Tall and slender, with short dark hair and the bluest eyes I have ever seen, she is truly a striking woman. Although not a classic beauty, still, there is something about her that exudes confidence and combined with her manners and deportment, the end result is a woman who seemed capable of holding her own with anyone – even Holmes.

"Am I your last visit, Mr. Holmes?" she inquired lightly.

Holmes smiled and said, "I had heard that you were well-informed."

"I do my best," she said. "However, I am certain that my circle of informants are no match for your, what do you call them? The Irregulars?"

"I am certain that yours are their equal; they just move in different circles," he said.

Holmes then repeated his tale about the ring of counterfeiters preying upon museums and collectors. When he had finished, he looked at her, and there was a long pause. Finally, I broke the uncomfortable silence saying, "I enjoyed your speech the other night. How did you become so interested in antiques?"

Ignoring Holmes, she spoke directly to me saying, "Collecting was my late husband's passion. I accompanied him on several expeditions to various countries, and I like to think that I not only retained a great deal of what he taught me but acquired a degree of expertise on my own."

Holmes then asked, "Do you authenticate the museum's purchases yourself?"

She laughed and said, "Heavens no. We have experts in various fields such as jewelry, ceramics, and weapons with whom we consult before we even consider tendering a bid."

"Are the other board members as knowledgeable as you?"

"You have interviewed two of them, Mr. Holmes, and you are related to the third, so I think that you are more than capable of answering your own question."

We chatted for a few more moments, and then Holmes said, "I do have another appointment." Pulling out his watch, I saw the fob fall to the floor a third time.

Lady Cox picked it up and examined it before returning it to my friend. "What an unusual piece," she said. "Are you familiar with the term *plique à jour,* Mr. Holmes?"

"Not really," replied Holmes. "I came across this piece in a pawn shop several years ago and was struck by the vibrant color. What is *plique à jour?*" he asked, deliberately mangling the pronunciation.

Lady Cox gave him a brief history, and concluded with, "But that could hardly be an example. True *plique à jour* is quite fragile, and I am certain, if it were genuine, it would have shattered upon striking the floor."

With that we bid Lady Cox adieu, and a minute or two later we were standing in front of her home. "It's a splendid afternoon, Watson. What say we stroll to Baker Street and try to work up an appetite for supper?"

I agreed and as we walked along in front of Regent's Park, I said to Holmes, "It would appear that the only person on the museum board who actually knows her business is Lady Cox."

"At first blush, I would be inclined to agree with you. However, we both know that appearances can be deceiving."

"What was that business with your watch fob constantly falling off? And when did you acquire a fob that resembles a piece of *plique à jour?* I seem to recall you having a sovereign with some sentimental value – not that you would ever admit to feeling sentimental – as your preferred *accoutrement.*"

"Surely you can see right through that bit of subterfuge. I merely secured the piece of glass with a slip knot that was tied to my vest pocket so that every time I removed the watch, the fob would fall."

"To what end?"

"I wanted to see what type of reaction, if any, the glass elicited from the board members."

"And?"

"You were there. You saw how they responded. Did anything strike you as unusual?"

By this time we had turned onto Baker Street, and from a distance, I heard a boy's voice bellowing, "Mr. 'Olmes! Mr. 'Olmes!" With that I spotted Wiggins running towards us as fast as his legs could carry him.

He pulled up, gasping for breath, but managed to utter, "We found 'im, Mr. 'Olmes. We found and followed that Roberts fella."

Chapter 12

"You've done well, Wiggins!" Holmes exclaimed. "Now then, take it easy, lad. Get your breath and then begin at the beginning and give me as many details as you can possibly recall."

Wiggins then informed us that he had been outside the studio of Dr. Wojno, and he had seen several customers enter the premises. However, late in the afternoon, she followed one particular fellow out, wiped her forehead as had been pre-arranged and then bid the man, "Good day."

Wiggins had then followed the man to a home in Mayfair. "Two of the boys, Frankie and Tom, are keepin' an eye on the place, Mr. 'Olmes."

"I want him watched around the clock," said Holmes. "If he goes out, have the boys follow – but at a distance. This Roberts may be a very dangerous fellow."

"Don't you worry 'bout us, guv. We 'as ways to take care of ourselves."

I was tempted to ask exactly what Wiggins meant but decided against it. Reaching into his wallet, Holmes extracted a few notes. "Make sure the boys eat well, and those that stay up all night should get a little something extra. Remember, Wiggins, be very careful, but make certain that he is always under surveillance. I will be expecting regular reports, and if anything happens, you are to summon me – no matter what the hour."

"Yes, sir!" exclaimed the boy who then scurried away down Baker Street almost as fast as he had run to us.

As you might expect, I was a bit taken aback. "Aren't you going to confront him? Don't you want to ask him about Prescott and Boles?"

"Confront him – and say what, old friend? I believe you are involved in one murder, possibly two. What do you have to say for yourself? No, it won't do, Watson. Let us watch Mr.

Roberts for a bit and see where he leads us. In this case, discretion truly is the better part of valor.

"Besides, I want to visit Dr. Wojno in the morning and see why Roberts was calling upon her. Would you care to join me?"

Of course I said yes, and early the next morning, after we had eaten a light breakfast, Holmes hailed a cab and we headed once again for Lambeth. As we entered the building that housed Dr. Wojno's workshop, I saw Holmes cast a discreet wave at a youngster.

Once again the bell had tinkled, signaling the arrival of a visitor, and once again Dr. Wojno emerged from the back room. "Oh, Mr. Holmes, I am delighted to see you. I thought you might come by yesterday."

"I did not receive the message until late in the day. My apologies. Now, I understand Mr. Roberts paid you a visit. May I ask what he wanted?"

"He brought me two molds and enough gold to fashion the three items that he had requested."

"The gold, may I see it?"

"I'm afraid I have already melted several pieces in the furnace. However, I have a few pieces that haven't been touched."

With that she disappeared into the back room, and she returned carrying two sets of gold candlestick holders."

"The pieces you melted down?"

"There were two cups and two plates. Mr. Roberts said he had acquired them at various pawn shops."

"And what exactly did he ask you to make?"

"Let me show you," she said, and with that she ushered us into her back room. Going to her work bench, she picked up two molds that appeared to be made of iron. "He wanted two of these," she said, indicating the first mold, "and one of these."

Holmes picked them up and examined them carefully. I could see that one was longer and thinner than the other, but I had no idea exactly what they were.

"And did he say when he would return to pick up the finished products?"

"He told me they had to be ready within a week. He said that he would pick them up next Friday at seven o'clock in the evening."

"Did he ask you to fashion anything else? Perhaps some additional glass pieces?"

"How could you possibly know that?" she asked.

"It is my business to know such things," Holmes explained. After he had paused for a moment, he continued, "Well then, Dr. Wojno, I would suggest that you begin their construction, but please let me know as soon as you have finished. Simply step outside your shop and walk to the post box on the corner. Then repeat the action as though you had forgot a second letter. Rest assured, the message will reach me."

"That's all I have to do?"

"Yes, aside from that, just go about your business as you normally would and leave the rest in my hands."

"As you wish, Mr. Holmes."

When we had exited the shop, I turned to Holmes and said, "I do hope you are not putting that young lady's life in any danger."

"I rather doubt it, Watson. They need her, you see. Their plans will not come to fruition without her continued contributions, albeit unknowing ones."

"But what exactly are their plans?"

"Surely, you have tumbled to that by now."

I looked at Holmes sheepishly and confessed my ignorance.

"Well, truth be told, it is a rather convoluted plot, but the fact remains that once you see things as they are and remove all the distractions, I think it becomes rather obvious," he added.

I let Holmes carry on, knowing full well he would enlighten me when he felt the time was right. In the interim, there was little for me to do but possess my soul in patience. At that moment, for some inexplicable reason, Milton crept into my mind. I suddenly found myself thinking about his blindness and my benightedness, and I decided that the poet was correct when he wrote, "They also serve who only stand and wait."

Truth be told, waiting was never one of my strengths. By contrast, however, it suited Holmes perfectly.

Holmes then hailed a cab and directed the driver to St. Etheldreda's Church. "Although I know candlesticks and a paten were taken, I've been meaning to pay a call upon Father Griffin to see if he might be able to shed any additional light on the matter and to see if he is aware of any other thefts in nearby churches."

Father Jack Griffin was an amiable sort. Stocky with a full beard and moustache and a head of brown hair that was beginning to gray at the temples, he looked like an athlete. After Holmes had introduced us, he congratulated the priest upon his recent promotion, and then asked about the theft. "Exactly, what was taken, Father?"

"They made off with two gold candlesticks that had been bequeathed to the church by the McDaid family and a chalice and paten that were a gift in remembrance of the late Cornelius Fitzpatrick, who had been a sexton of the church."

"And these items, they were all made of solid gold?"

"Indeed, they were," replied the priest.

"Have you any idea when the theft occurred?"

"Sometime between nine and noon," replied the priest.

"How can you be so certain?"

"I celebrated mass on that altar at eight that morning, and I planned to celebrate a noon mass there as well, but when I returned, I noticed that they were missing."

"Anything else that you can recall about the theft?"

The clergyman thought for a moment and then he smiled, "Well, it may be nothing, but I recall thinking it was rather odd at the time."

"What's that?" inquired Holmes.

"The candlesticks and paten were taken from a side altar, but if they had looked behind them, they would have seen a pair of silver candlestick holders on the opposite side of the church. I suppose they were in too much of a hurry to make off with their goods. I will say a prayer for them."

"Yes, I am certain you are right," replied Holmes. We then bade Father Griffin good-day, and having left the semi-darkness of the church behind and emerged into a beautifully sunny day, we decided to walk back to Baker Street.

We had gone but a few steps when Holmes turned to me and said, "What do you make of it, Watson?"

"I am certain Father Griffin was correct. After they had what they came for, they left as soon as possible."

"That's certainly possible, but why leave the other candlestick holders?"

"Perhaps they didn't see them," I offered.

"So then this was just a crime of opportunity rather than a carefully planned theft?"

"I should think so, but obviously you disagree."

"I am inclined to think that our thief or thieves were given very specific instructions. Orders so precise that they dare not deviate from them – even to enrich themselves. Consider, they had to examine all the altars to locate the candles, yet they took only the gold, leaving the silver behind."

"To what end?" I was becoming exasperated, and the thought that Holmes could see beyond what I had ascertained and yet refused to share was a trifle stinging.

"I know if I were to say, 'In good time,' it would only drive you further to distraction, so consider this." Holmes then outlined in great detail exactly what he was thinking, and when he had finished, I was, to say the least, stunned.

"Holmes, that is abominable," I exclaimed. "It simply cannot be the case."

"I agree that it is a despicable plan," he replied, "but, for the present, the events I have outlined to you offer the only explanation that suits all the facts which we possess. Now, if the situation should change, we will revisit and most certainly revise this line of thought. However, it will do for the present."

"What is your next move?"

"I think it is long past due that we had a conversation with Mr. Roberts. I am just trying to decide where and when so that we have the deck stacked in our favor as it were. Now, let me consider the possibilities for a bit."

Although I continued to pepper him with questions, he remained resolute and would comment no further on his plans.

It was only after we had arrived at our lodgings, and he was enjoying a pipe before supper that he turned to me and said, "As soon as I receive a full report from Wiggins, I shall let you know how we are going to approach Mr. Roberts. I have devised two scenarios – both have distinct advantages, so I must wait to hear from the lads to see if one outshines the other."

Little happened over the next few days. Holmes received regular reports from Wiggins or one of the other Irregulars, and then late Wednesday afternoon, word arrived that Dr. Wojno had given the signal that the work was completed.

The next morning we breakfasted early, hailed a cab and Holmes directed the driver to take us to the address in Lambeth. We entered the shop, and Dr. Wojno greeted us. "I finished only yesterday," she said, "and I gave the sign immediately."

"May I see the final products?" asked Holmes.

She nodded and led us into the work area. Reaching beneath a bench, she withdrew two small wooden chests. As she opened them, I saw that one contained two small goblets complete with ornate tops while the other housed a round golden plate. Extracting a handkerchief from his pocket, Holmes picked up one of the goblets. Turning to me, he said, "Look familiar, Watson?"

"Why, it's almost the same size as the Mérode Cup, only without the *plique à jour*."

"Exactly," he said. He replaced the cup carefully and then turned his attention to the platter. He withdrew his lens from his pocket and examined it carefully. Turning back to Dr. Wojno, he asked, "Do you have the approximate dimensions?"

"It is just a bit under five inches," she replied.

"Just so," he said. "And the glass pieces?"

"Right here," she replied, holding up a small black velvet sack with a gold drawstring.

"You have done well, and I hope that very soon, you can put this sad chapter behind you and continue with your celestial aspirations."

Outside, Holmes looked at me and said, "This grows more brazen with each new discovery that we make."

Hailing a cab, Holmes directed the driver to take us to the nearest telegraph office. After sending two wires, he returned to the cab and said, "If I am correct, and I fear I am, the way forward from here is dark and treacherous. From this moment on, we must not let our guard down – even for a second."

We headed back to Baker Street, where Holmes summoned one of his street urchins before we entered our rooms. I couldn't hear what his instructions to the lad were, but no sooner had Holmes finished than the boy sprinted off down Baker Street in the direction of Marylebone Road.

After we had settled ourselves in our chairs, Holmes began the ritual of preparing his pipe. He had finished one pipe and had just finished filling it with tobacco for a second time, when the bell rang loudly, and a minute later we heard the clatter of young feet ascending the stairs. No sooner had the first knock sounded than Holmes yelled, "Come in, Wiggins."

The lad entered and said, "I have news, Mr. 'Olmes. Mr. Roberts sent a wire to Dr. Wojno telling 'er that 'e'd be there at noon tomorrow."

"Splendid, Wiggins. Keep the lads outside her shop through the night, and there will be no need to follow Mr. Roberts tomorrow."

"No?"

"No. Dr. Watson and I will keep an eye on Roberts as soon as he leaves the glassmaker's shop. Follow him only if you don't see us on the scene tomorrow at noon."

"Righto, Mr. 'Olmes. How will I know if you are there?"

"We will be in a Clarence about a block away."

107

And so it was that the next day at half eleven, we were sitting in an enclosed carriage close to Dr. Wojno's factory waiting for the mysterious Roberts to arrive. At about five to the hour, a hansom pulled up in front of the shop and a tall, thin man descended from the carriage, spoke to the driver and entered the shop. He had been gone but two minutes when a youngster approached the hansom and spoke to the driver. A minute later, the cab departed.

"You arranged that, didn't you?"

"Of course," replied Holmes. "I anticipated his arrival and then holding the cab. After all, they are not nearly so plentiful here as on the other side of the bridge. Now, Watson, let's switch seats. I want Roberts to think this cab is empty and available."

So we sat in silence for several minutes and then I heard a male voice inquire, "Are you free?"

The cab lurched forward, and a minute later, the man I saw going into the shop started to enter our carriage. He was carrying a small Gladstone bag and had settled into the seat facing us before his eyes had adjusted to the darkness and he realized that he was not alone.

"I beg your pardon," he began, "but I was under the impression that this cab was free."

"I don't mind sharing a cab, if you don't," said Holmes with an air of magnanimity.

"That's very decent of you," said Roberts. "Where are you headed?"

"Marylebone Road," said Holmes. "And you?"

"I have an appointment in Wembley, so we can just drop you gentlemen off, and I will continue on my way. Since my destination is the more distant and you have been kind enough to share, I insist that you let me pay the fare."

"You are too kind," I said.

"I wouldn't dream of such a thing," replied Holmes. "We shall split the fare in half. After all, your company is far more valuable than a few shillings," said Holmes.

"Oh, what makes you say that? After all, you just met me."

"Yes, but I know of you, Mr. Roberts."

Although the man looked startled, he quickly regained his composure. "You have the advantage of me, sir."

"Yes, I suppose I do. I have quite forgot my manners. My name is Sherlock Holmes and this is my colleague, Dr. John Watson."

As you might expect, when Holmes uttered his name, it had quite an effect on our companion. Even in the dim light of the cab, I could swear I saw him blanch. However, I must say that he quickly regained his composure even as Holmes continued, "I see my name is familiar to you."

"You are known far and wide, Mr. Holmes. I must say this is certainly an unexpected honour and a pleasure, I might add."

"I wonder if you will feel the same when you are sharing a cell with some other ne'er-do-well at Newgate – assuming, of course, that you can avoid the noose."

"What on Earth are you talking about, Mr. Holmes? I have done nothing wrong."

Holmes leaned back and smiled, first at Roberts and then at me. "Nothing wrong?" As he recited the next part, Holmes ticked the various offenses off on his fingers. "Nothing wrong?" he repeated. "I suppose you know nothing of fake artifacts being sold to museums and collectors? Thus it follows that you would be ignorant of the death of Ralph Prescott. Continuing that line of thought, you would then be totally in the dark regarding the murder of Chester Boles.

"No, no, Mr. Roberts, I'm afraid it will not do. You are in it up to your neck. It just remains to be determined whether you are the prime mover or a mere underling, sent out to do the bidding of your betters."

Roberts had grown more agitated as Holmes continued to speak. Finally, he lost all control and fairly shrieked, "You dare to refer to me as an underling? You, the Scotland Yard lapdog? Always sticking your nose where it isn't wanted. Here's a thought, Mr. Holmes, suppose I shoot you and your colleague right now?" With that he withdrew a silver-plated derringer from his coat pocket and aimed it squarely at Holmes' chest.

"I hardly think that will do you much good," Holmes said easily. "Doctor Watson never goes anywhere without his service revolver and I am certain he has it trained on you as we speak. Moreover, there is a carriage directly behind us carrying both Inspector Lestrade and Inspector Gregson of Scotland Yard. No, Mr. Roberts, I would say the best course for you is to cooperate and throw yourself on the mercy of the court."

"I suppose you are right, Mr. Holmes," wailed Roberts, who then sank to his knees in front of Holmes and me and began to beg for forgiveness. I leaned forward to console the man and suddenly felt the metal of the gun barrel against my chest.

Roberts turned to Holmes and said, "It's easy to be cavalier with your own life, Mr. Holmes. I'm wondering if you are willing to play so fast and loose with your companion's well-being."

Holmes looked at him and said, "If you harm Watson ..."

"No one will come to any harm if you just do what I say." He then called for the driver to stop the cab and he ordered Holmes out. "If there is indeed a hansom filled with police officers following us – something I'm rather inclined to doubt – tell them to stop or your friend's life is forfeit."

After Holmes had alighted from the cab, Roberts instructed the driver to proceed to Victoria Station. He then had me remove my braces, which he cut in half. He bound my ankles and wrists and tied a handkerchief around my mouth as a gag.

After we had reached Victoria, he told the driver I wasn't feeling well and that he should take me to 221B Baker Street. He then paid the fare, and the last I saw of him, he was bowing to me with a smirk on his face before he turned and entered the train station.

Chapter 13

I was sitting in my chair when I heard the front door open and Holmes bound up the stairs. He rushed into the room and seemed quite relieved to find me on the sofa.

I explained how Roberts had bound me, exited from the cab at Victoria and instructed the driver to take me to 221B. "When we arrived, and I didn't alight, the driver opened the roof door and upon seeing me bound, promptly released me. I knew you would return here shortly, so I have been awaiting your arrival."

"What a curious turn of events," remarked Holmes. "He might have held you for ransom or at the very least used you for leverage to dissuade me from my investigations. Instead, he sends you home safe and sound – albeit bound."

"What does it mean, Holmes? And what does this say about the character of Roberts? In addition to his pistol, he had a knife. Once he had me bound and helpless, he could have stabbed me or slit my throat, but he told the driver to take me home. He even paid the fare as he said he would."

"This will definitely require some thought," he said as he threw himself into his chair and began filling his black clay pipe with shag. That he had chosen the black one, long his favorite, told me that this might well be what he liked to describe as another "three-pipe problem."

Knowing that any attempts to engage him in conversation would prove futile and that the room would soon be a miasma of thick smoke unsuitable for anyone's lungs, I decided to dine at my club. On the way out, I told Mrs. Hudson she need not prepare dinner for me. I also cautioned her that Holmes was in one of his "thoughtful" moods and suggested she prepare a light dinner and attempt to deliver it as late as possible. Being as aware of my friend's eccentricities as I, she thanked me and promised to heed my advice.

We were both well-aware that when he was deeply involved in a case, Holmes gave little if any thought to food.

It was after ten when I finally returned home. The room had been aired, and both windows were half open. I could only assume that was the work of our landlady. Holmes, however, was nowhere to be found.

Nor did he appear the next morning at breakfast. By midday I was beginning to worry and considered making Lestrade aware of my missing friend when I heard the front door open and a moment later Holmes strode into the room with a slight smile on his face.

"Judging by your expression, you have made some progress on the case."

"Indeed, I have," he replied. "It took some time, and I cannot believe what a dullard I have been. Fortunately, I think that I have salvaged this case and prevented it from being an abject failure. Although I will never count it among my successes, either."

"What on Earth do you mean?"

"We, or more accurately I, have been looking at this from the wrong angle."

"Oh?" I must admit that at this point I had no idea what Holmes was talking about nor where this conversation was headed.

"Consider, we have a dead antiquarian and a slain jeweler. Surely, the deaths must be related. After all, the courier, Prescott, was carrying *plique à jour* samples as well as a diamond that is either an antique or has been cut to resemble one.

"And the jeweler, Boles, also appeared to be crafting antique pieces as evidenced by the tools and sketches in his workshop."

"What sketches?" I exclaimed. "You have not mentioned any such drawings up until now."

"Oh, haven't I?" said Holmes innocently. "I found them during a nocturnal visit to Boles' shop. They were hidden behind two engravings that hung in his back office."

"Well, that would certainly seem to tie the two together."

"I agree, but what if there were another connection – one that was not so obvious, one that might require a bit of digging and a stretch of the imagination."

"And have you found such a link?"

"Not yet, but I am working on it, and I believe I have taken a few small steps toward forging the other connection that links those two."

"And would you care to enlighten me?"

"Not just yet, old friend. I am still untangling the threads that formed this pattern. However, you may rest assured that as soon as I have accomplished that feat you shall be the first to know.

"By the way, Watson. Are you free this evening? I am planning an excursion and would appreciate your company if you are so disposed."

"Holmes, I am always at your service; you know that."

"Good old Watson. I should be lost without you – the one fixed point in an ever-changing universe.

"By the way, it's formal dress so be ready by ten. And if you can manage it, do bring your revolver. I would only ask that you make every attempt to make its presence as inconspicuous as possible."

The last remark was thrown over his shoulder as he entered his bedroom. As you might expect, I was more than a bit nonplussed, given such seemingly contradictory requests, but I resolved to soldier on and carry out Holmes' command to the best of my ability.

In this instance, I was one step ahead of my friend. During his extended absence the previous three years I had purchased my own Webley Bull Dog as it fit better into my medical bag and weighed a great deal less. With its shorter barrel, I thought it would suit Holmes' preferences to a tee. Retiring to my own room, I spent the rest of the afternoon cleaning and oiling it. Since I expected to be out late, I decided a nap would also be in order, and I was only awakened by the gentle tapping of Mrs. Hudson on my door. She had come to tell that "dinner was ready" and that "Mr. Holmes would be returning presently."

I dined alone on a savory shepherd's pie. After dinner I waited for Holmes, but when he had not returned at nine, I went up to my room to change. I was nearly finished when I heard Holmes enter below. I descended to find my friend already dressed and looking quite debonair.

"Where are we going, Holmes? And why all the secrecy?"

"Just a little more patience, Watson," he replied and with that he entered his room and returned immediately carrying a paper sack.

We then descended the stairs and entered an enclosed carriage that was waiting for us.

"Holmes, you are just full of tricks today."

"The evening is young, Doctor."

"May I ask where we are going?"

"You are aware there are any number of secret societies in London?"

"Of course," I replied, "The Freemasons and the Rosicrucians come to mind immediately."

"There are others," replied Holmes. "One of the newest being The Hermetic Order of the Golden Dawn, which came into being just a few years ago."

"Is that where we are headed?"

"No, we are going to a very special meeting of the *Wunderschönen Techni.*"

"Never heard of it," I protested.

"I would be surprised if you had," replied my friend. "Its existence is one of the most closely guarded secrets – both here and abroad."

"*Wunderschönen Techni*? What does it mean? What do the members do?"

"The name is a curious mix of German and Greek which can be translated as 'beautiful art.' Its members are collectors, and they are willing to pay for pieces to add to their collections. If the seller can prove the provenance, all other questions are immaterial."

"Are you saying they traffic in stolen goods?"

"To a degree – some items have been liberated from their owners while others are sold by their owners."

"But why secret?"

"There are many reasons, Watson. In the case of stolen items, I should think no explanation is necessary. In other instances, the owners have fallen on hard times. I've been given to understand that the right pieces can fetch far more here than they might at the best auction houses.

"Selling them on the sly also allows the seller to keep up appearances. He can replace the original with a clever forgery and few, if any, are the wiser. Best of all, these auctions command far less of a commission than their more legitimate counterparts."

"How long have you known about these …auctions?"

"I have been aware of their existence, in one form or another, for several years. I have never had occasion to attend one until now. By the way, that reminds me." With that, he opened the paper sack he had been carrying and reached in and pulled out two elaborate masks such as might be seen in a *commedia dell'arte.* "Your choice, Doctor. Would you prefer the Bauta mask or the *Dottore Peste?* I assure you, I have no preference."

"Does everyone wear these?"

"Indeed. Although underground, these are still affairs of high society and given their illicit transactions, it is better for all if no one knows who each other is."

"I think I should prefer the *Dottore* mask, the other will completely cover your face.

"Indeed," he smiled. And one more thing, he reached inside his coat pocket and withdrew a black feather."

"Is that…?"

He cut me off. "You remember that Prescott had one of these with him. It took me some time, but I was finally able to ascertain that these feathers are the tokens which allow individuals to move from the ballroom to the auction room."

"This grows increasingly strange with each passing moment."

"Not really, Watson. The ravens were sacred to Odin but they were also used as messengers by Apollo in Greek mythology hence the bilingual name which this group has adopted."

By this time, we were down by the Thames when our carriage suddenly stopped in front of a warehouse.

"The docks?" I queried.

"Far away from the police and virtually deserted at night – rather ideal for such a clandestine gathering, I should think," Holmes replied. "Now, do put on your mask and let us see what the evening brings."

We entered a rather cavernous building and I was surprised to see perhaps one hundred people inside. The gentlemen were all attired in evening dress while the women were sporting extravagant ball gowns. As you might expect, everyone's face was concealed by an elaborate mask. Despite that precaution I am certain I recognized one or two individuals, but propriety forbids me from naming them.

I followed Holmes to a door in the rear where two large fellows stood guard. "I'm sorry, sir, but this room is off-limits this evening," said one.

"Not for me," replied Holmes lightly, pulling his raven's feather from his jacket.

"My apologies, sir," said the burly fellow as he opened the portal for Holmes.

Turning to me, he said, "Will you be attending as well?"

"I should think so," I replied, showing him my own feather.

He then favored me with a polite half-bow and said, "Enjoy your evening, sir."

This new room was considerably smaller, and there were far fewer people in attendance – perhaps 20 at most. They were seated at small tables and enjoying beverages that were being served by masked waiters.

"The auction has already started," hissed Holmes.

At that, I turned my attention to the front where I saw a man standing on a polished wood podium. To his left was a small table and to his right was an easel.

"Ladies and gentlemen, our next item is an exquisite piece – 'Justinian Drafting His Laws,' an oil on canvas by Eugene Delacroix. I would like an opening bid of £5,000."

Immediately a woman sitting to my right raised her hand. As the bidding continued, I turned to Holmes and said, "I thought that painting was lost during a fire at the Paris Commune."

He merely shrugged and said, "Apparently, you and the rest of the world were misinformed, for as you can see, it survived the inferno and has been residing in the country estate of a French nobleman who has since fallen on hard times."

"My word!" At that point the bidding concluded and the woman who had started the bidding ended up with the high bid of £11,000."

The next three items were all paintings that had disappeared or were believed lost to various calamities. Holmes knew the history of each and related them to me. Although I found them mildly interesting, I will not bore you with the sordid details of each.

"Our final item consists of two German *fibulae*, believed to date from the sixth century. I will now give interested parties a few moments to examine the items."

"Finally," said an exasperated Holmes. "This is the item I have been waiting for. Unfortunately, as you might expect, Watson, there are no catalogues, nor are there previews of any sort. I shall return presently as I should like to examine them more closely."

I watched as Holmes made his way to the table where he and three or four other people were poring over the items. As I looked on, I saw a rather petite woman join Holmes and the others on the stage. She was wearing a brilliant red gown, and I thought, "I believe I know her." Unfortunately, I was unable to place her as an ornate gold and red cat mask concealed most of her face.

When he returned, I asked, "I know what a fibula is but what exactly is a *fibulae?*"

"That would be *fibula,* Doctor. As I'm sure you know, if you will recall your Latin, *fibulae* is the plural. Think of it as a brooch or clasp used to fasten a garment. I believe their use began with the Greeks."

"Does it have anything to do with the bone?"

"Excellent. There are some who believe the bone is so named because the shape it makes with the tibia resembles a clasp, with the fibula serving as the pin."

"Holmes, you never cease to amaze me,"

Indicating the items at the front of the room, he said, "Those are outstanding examples. They are bejeweled, and unless I am much mistaken, they were destined for the Kunsthistorisches Museum, currently under construction in Vienna."

"Then how did they end up here?"

"I am certain the Emperor Franz Joseph would be wondering the same thing were he here, and if we knew the answer to that, I think we should also know who killed Prescott and Boles. However, we are making progress.

"Had I the funds, I should very much like to bid on those *fibulae,* but they are beyond my means."

"I wish I could help," I replied. "Perhaps you can wire Mycroft for a loan."

Holmes looked at me curiously then he let out with a dry sardonic chuckle and said, "Come, Watson. I've seen everything I need to see here. A few well-placed wires in the morning might go a long way toward answering that question and shedding some light upon the problem that confronts us at present."

As we were leaving, I heard the auctioneer say, "They are exquisite are they not, ladies and gentlemen? So let us start with an opening bid of £2,000. Very good. Do I hear £2,500?"

When we were safely in the hansom and heading for Baker Street, I said to Holmes, "There was a woman in a red dress who joined you on stage…"

"So you noticed her as well?"

"Given that gown, it was difficult to miss her. But why was she there?"

"Truth be told, Doctor, she is the reason we were there." After that pronouncement, he dropped his head to his chest, and we spent the rest of the ride in silence.

Chapter 14

When I made my way downstairs the next morning, I was surprised to see Holmes sitting in his chair, reading *The Times*. "You're up early," I said.

"I have been up for some two hours," he replied. "I have dispatched several telegrams, written three letters and enjoyed two cups of coffee."

"If I didn't know better, I'd think you had made progress on the case."

"I believe that I have. I am waiting for a reply to one of my wires that will confirm it."

"Shall we sit here all day and bide our time?"

"Eat your breakfast. If my reply has not arrived by the time you have finished, I believe I know a way that we can engage ourselves for the better part of the day."

As I filled my stomach with scrambled eggs and bacon, I perused my copy of *The Daily Telegraph*. I was struck by an article stating that the Kensington Museum planned to exchange a number of pieces with The Louvre.

"Are you aware of this proposed transaction?" I asked after I had read the pertinent details to Holmes.

"Actually, it is a fairly common practice, and it benefits both parties," Holmes said. "Think of it as changing casts in an opera. You might be inclined to return to see a new mezzo soprano perform in *Carmen*. Having seen Celestine Galli-Marie, who created the role, I should dearly love to see Adelina Patti on stage so that I might compare the two. Man craves variety, so museums are constantly adding, subtracting and exchanging portions of their collections in order to attract new visitors."

"I suppose you are right."

At that moment, there was a knock on the door, "Come in Mrs. Hudson," Holmes said.

Our landlady entered, "These just arrived for you, Mr. Holmes. Thinking they might be important, I brought them up immediately."

Jumping to his feet, Holmes thanked our landlady and as soon as she had departed, he tore open the first envelope. He perused it twice before handing it to me, "It is as I suspected, Watson."

I looked down at the short message:'

"All fibulae accounted for at Kunsthistorisches Museum."

"Well, surely that is good news," I replied. "Nothing is missing which means nothing has been stolen."

"You miss the point, old man. Consider carefully what that telegram implies and then draw your own inferences." As he said that, he opened the second envelope, this new communiqué seemed to hold his attention a bit longer. Finally, he laughed rather drily and said, "Odd, you don't know what to make of that telegram while I am uncertain what to make of this one."

With that he handed me the second telegram. I gazed at its contents and then said simply, "What the devil?"

Taking the telegram back from me, Holmes read it again, and then he read it aloud.

"Mr. Holmes, you must cease before things take a most unpleasant turn."

"No signature," I stated.

"Rather to be expected," replied Holmes.

"I must confess that I am at a loss as to how to proceed."

"Fortunately, Watson, I am not. Now, I have a number of tasks to which I must attend. If you are free, perhaps we can meet for lunch at Goldini's. Say, two o'clock?"

"I'll be there," I promised.

With that, Holmes donned his coat and hat and descended the stairs. I went to the window where I watched him hail a cab and he headed off in the direction of Regent's Park. With an entire morning to myself, I set about catching up on my correspondence and had just begun organizing the notes from one of our earliest cases – the mysterious death of Sir Geoffrey Malory who was found dead in his locked study on New Year's Day, 1881 – when I heard the bell ring.

A minute or two later, I heard a gentle rapping on the door, which I recognized as that of our landlady. Refusing to bellow across the room, I went to the door and opened it. Mrs. Hudson was standing there, holding a card.

"A gentleman has called to see Mr. Holmes."

"He went out earlier," I said.

"Oh, I must have been at the market, for I didn't see him leave." With that she handed me the card, and I was rather surprised to see that it bore the name Sir Edward Hargreaves, the director of the South Kensington Museum.

"You may tell him that Mr. Holmes is out, but that I shall relay his message to Holmes as soon as possible. In the interim, I would be more than happy to try to assist him in any way possible."

A minute later, Sir Edward entered the room. After introducing myself, I explained that Holmes was unavailable at the moment. "Is there any way I may be of assistance?"

"I know that you work closely with Mr. Holmes, so I shall explain my situation to you, If you can't see any solution, then you may pass along my plea to Mr. Holmes. As you might expect, Dr. Watson, time may not be our friend in this situation."

I showed Sir Edward to a seat and then asked Mrs. Hudson to prepare a pot of tea. He was as nervous as cat, so I offered him a cigarette which he declined, pulling out a cigar case from his jacket pocket and asking if I minded. I said of course not and then lit his and my own before asking him to proceed.

"Sir, since I have no idea to what 'situation' you make reference, I can only encourage you, as Mr. Holmes would do, to begin at the beginning and to omit nothing. Even the smallest detail may prove significant."

"I shall do my best," said Hargreaves. "I believe that something is amiss at the museum."

"Can you be a little more specific?"

"I wish that I could, Doctor. It is a feeling I have that I simply cannot escape."

"Perhaps you can shed some light on the origin of the feeling?" I suggested.

"Last week, I was examining some of the items in the medieval gallery — it is my personal favorite — and I was left with the distinct impression that several of them had been moved."

"Moved? In what way?"

At that moment, Mrs. Hudson entered with the tea and we continued our conversation after I had poured cups for both of us.

"As I was saying, Doctor, in one display case, there were several bracteates. You know what they are?"

"I do indeed," I replied.

"Excellent! Well they seemed to have been rearranged. There's one with an eagle that was always on top. I say that because one day I whimsically thought of it as flying above all the others. Only when I looked at the exhibit last week, the eagle was now in the middle, and the topmost spot was occupied by a medal that featured two crossed swords."

"How very odd? Is this the first time this has happened?"

"It's the first time I'm absolutely certain something has been moved. I've had a similar feeling on several occasions in the past."

"And the workers?"

"All the workers, from the curator down to the guards have denied moving the bracteates."

"Well, I shall certainly inform Mr. Holmes of your concerns, and I am certain that he will be in touch."

With that Sir Edward departed, and it wasn't until just before dinner that I heard Holmes' footfalls on the stairs. I had completely forgot our plans for lunch, which either Holmes had forget as well or was kind enough not to mention.

After he had hung up his coat and hat, I exclaimed, "Holmes, I am so glad that you are home."

"Did you have a nice visit with Sir Edward?" he asked as he settled into his chair and lit a cigarette.

"How could you possibly know he was here?"

"The two teacups on the sideboard tell me you have had a visitor."

"Yes, but it could have been anyone. How the deuce could you know Sir Edward has been here?"

"Surely you can smell the lingering aroma of the Por Larrañaga which I'm assuming he enjoyed. And if that weren't enough, there is the ash," he said pointing to the floor ashtray where Hargreaves had tipped the ash from the cigar.

"My word, Holmes. You are amazing."

"Not really, Watson. I saw Hargreaves smoking a Por Larrañaga – not a terribly common cigar – at the recent benefit, and the rest is simplicity itself."

"At any rate, Hargreaves is having misgivings about some goings-on at the museum."

"Do tell," said Holmes.

I then proceeded to relate the conversation between Hargreaves and myself to Holmes, who had sat back in his chair, with his knees drawn up, eyes closed and fingers steepled under his chin. It was a familiar pose and one he often adopted when he was giving his undivided attention to something or simply wished to reason through a thorny problem.

When I finished, he sat there in silence. Not wishing to disturb his train of thought, I remained in my seat as well. Fully several minutes later, Holmes looked at me and said, "What did you gather from Hargreaves' report?"

"It would appear someone is sneaking into the museum at night and tinkering with the displays."

He cast me a baleful look before he said, "Tinkering? Surely you can do better than that, Watson."

"Rearranging the displays? But to what end?"

"How about substituting items, Doctor. One newly fashioned bracteate or plate or cup for an old one. Much like the sorcerer tricked Aladdin's wife in the *Arabian Nights* – only these new artifacts are worthless by comparison to the originals – just as the new lamp was when compared to Aladdin's priceless treasure."

"But surely someone would have noticed," I exclaimed.

"Doctor, why do people go to museums?"

"To see the exhibits, of course."

126

"Exactly! To see but not to observe. If the forgery is well-executed – and these are – then we believe what we see. So if the information card tells us we are looking at the Royal Cup or the Mérode Cup, we look and we admire and we move on – but do we question? I think not."

"Holmes, are you saying all the items in the museums are counterfeits?"

"Of course not, I'm merely suggesting that there may be more bogus items on display than you might suspect."

"What's to be done?"

"I do have a plan, Doctor, but it will require cooperation from some highly placed people and a bit of luck." Holmes then outlined his plan to me in broad strokes. When he had finished, I looked at him in amazement. Finally, after I had digested the scheme, I could only say, "Holmes, you would have made a most dangerous criminal."

His only response was a dry laugh, as he set about refilling his pipe, with just the hint of a smile playing across his saturnine features.

Chapter 15

The next morning we paid a visit to Mycroft at his office in Whitehall. I had met Mycroft on several previous occasions, the last, before this adventure, was when he had helped Holmes and me escape from Moriarty's henchmen.

To say he was surprised to see us would be something of an understatement. Still, despite being disturbed, he made a slight effort to be cordial. "I do hope this is a matter of some importance, brother. I am in the midst of trying to convince the Chancellor of the Exchequer that death duties might be a way to cope with the looming budget crisis."

"You want to tax people on their inheritance? Seems rather like kicking a man when he's down," I offered.

"I assure you, Doctor, I do not enjoy the prospect, but it is a necessary evil, unfortunately. One that will become even more so if the Ashanti continue down their wayward path. But I know you didn't come here to discuss foreign policy, so what is on your mind, Sherlock? Does it have anything to do with the museum?"

"Indeed it does," replied Holmes. "I think I have made considerable progress, but I fear this forgery ring may be far more intricate than either of us first imagined. To that end, I must request a small favor – one which I am certain you will be happy to grant."

"Another favor?" replied Mycroft, arching his eyebrows, "Wasn't the rumor about the Founder's Jewel enough?"

"That was certainly a help, but its benefits have yet to come to fruition. However, if you can see your way clear to granting this request, I think I may be able to bring everything to a satisfactory conclusion."

"What makes you so certain of that?"

"Because without your assistance, I may not be able to bring the ringleaders to justice and a murderer may well escape the gallows."

"And what exactly is it that you require from me?"

"I should like to borrow the Alfred Jewel from the Ashmolean Museum at Oxford."

For the second time in as many weeks, I thought I saw Mycroft taken aback. After composing himself, he chuckled – something he seldom did – and said: "Now you want more than a rumor, you want me to entrust you with one of England's oldest treasures, presumably to use as some sort of bait?"

"Exactly," replied Holmes, with an air of nonchalance which I am certain his brother must have found at least mildly off-putting.

"And if I should refuse?"

"Then you must find me an antique of similar value that is certain to appeal to a collector. Something from the Crown Jewels, perhaps," said Holmes. "the Coronation Spoon or the scepter of Mary II?"

"Out of the question," said Mycroft firmly. "Let me make a few discreet inquiries about the Alfred Jewel. I make no promises but you will hear from me shortly."

"If your calls should come to fruition, here are the other conditions surrounding the loan that may make it more palatable for all involved." With that Holmes reached into his inside jacket pocket and withdrew a piece of paper that had been folded in half. He handed it to Mycroft and said, "I believe that is all I require – for the moment."

Mycroft read the list, pausing once or twice to cast a wry look at his brother. "And if I am able to do these things?"

"Then with any luck, a scandal will be averted and a criminal will be brought to justice."

With that, we left Mycroft's office and stepped out into the bright late morning sun. "I think that went about as well as could be expected," chuckled Holmes.

"Do you really think Mycroft will be able to 'borrow' the, what was it, the Alfred Jewel?"

"I have no doubt of it," replied Holmes. "Are you not familiar with it, Watson?"

I shook my head, loath to acknowledge my ignorance.

"The Alfred Jewel was discovered in 1693, in North Petherton, Somerset. It is believed to have belonged to Alfred the Great, which would seem to date it from the late 9th century. It is inscribed with the words, AELFRED MEC HEHT GEWYRCAN, in the Old English alphabet, which can be translated as 'Alfred ordered me made.' It is constructed of enamel and quartz enclosed in gold and is generally regarded as an unusual example of Anglo-Saxon goldsmithing.

"Shaped something like a pear and at a mere two-and-a-half inches tall, it is rather small, which makes it ideal for our purpose."

"And what exactly is our purpose, in this instance?"

"In due time, old friend. I am still ironing out some of the details in my mind."

Knowing Holmes' flair for the dramatic, I decided not to press the issue. However, I must admit that I was more than a little concerned that my friend was willing to put a national treasure at risk in a plan that he had not yet finished formulating.

Still, it was but two days later in the afternoon that I heard the bell ring. "A client, perhaps?" I offered.

Holmes, who was standing at the window, watching the traffic on Baker Street, said, "I think not. I rather suspect it is a messenger from Mycroft."

As if on cue, Mrs. Hudson knocked on the door and Holmes bade her enter. "There's a young man requesting to see you, Mr. Holmes. He said he has a delivery for you."

"By all means, show him up."

A minute or two later, a man knocked on the door and Holmes again bade him enter. A strapping fellow, well-built with a head of curly blond hair and a hairbrush moustache entered. He nodded at me and then spoke to Holmes. "Mr. Holmes, I have been instructed to place this package in no one's hands but yours." With that he held out a small box for my friend to examine.

"Thank you, Mr. ..."

"Gibbons, sir. Also, your brother requested that you sign this receipt before I turn over the package."

Holmes looked at me and said, "I suppose fraternal trust does have its limits." He then took the paper to his chemistry table where he signed it and handed it to Gibbons, who in turn relinquished the box.

After wishing us a good day, Gibbons turned on his heel and left the room.

"Obviously, a former soldier," I said.

"I should think an officer," replied Holmes. "Consider his bearing, as well as the tie pin he wore."

"I saw no tie pin."

"It was half concealed by his waistcoat but I recognized the insignia for the officers of the Royal Engineers. He had taken a lapel badge and cleverly had it refashioned into a stick pin."

Turning his attention to the box, Holmes pulled out a penknife and cut the twine that secured it. He then tore off the paper. Sliding back the lid on a small wooden box, the inside of which had been carefully lined with red velvet, Holmes reached inside and held up the object therein as he announced, "The Alfred Jewel."

"And now that you have it, what will you do with it?"

"Search for a buyer, of course," he said.

"And how will you do that? I don't think an ad in *The Times* is advisable!"

"There's that pawky sense of humour that I so missed during my recent sojourn," he replied. "No, for that I shall require some assistance."

"Do you have anyone in mind?"

"Since she was at the auction the other night, I thought I might try to prevail upon Madame Pittorino."

"You mentioned that she was the reason we were at the auction. But how can you be so certain it was she? After all, there are many petite women in London. Given the fact that everyone was masked, how could you be certain it was she?"

"When we visited her shop, she was wearing a pair of small gold hoop earrings. I spotted those identical earrings on a woman at the auction."

"Was she wearing a red gown and a cat mask?"

"Bravo, Watson."

"I grant you the woman in the red gown certainly had Madame Pittorino's stature, but to hang it all on a pair of earrings."

"Don't forget the ring."

"What ring?"

"She was also wearing a small diamond ring on the fourth finger of her right hand when we visited her, and the woman in red was sporting an identical ring. I believe I have made my feelings known about coincidences."

He then sat at his desk and composed a brief note. Summoning the page, he handed him the envelope and instructed him to deliver it with all the speed he could muster and to wait for a reply. After the lad had left, I said, "I suppose that's a letter for Madame."

"Indeed it is. If I can enlist her on our side, it will go a long way toward lending the charade we must play a tint of credibility."

"What charade?"

"Well, I can't very well appear to any prospective buyer as myself, but if Madame Pittorino will vouch for me that will certainly lend credence to any *bona fides* I might dream up."

"Are you certain you can trust her? It seems to me there is a great deal at stake here."

"Again, I am not certain of anything, but one must begin somewhere. And now to another facet of this puzzle." With that he pulled out his violin and began to play. The sounds were surprisingly harsh and cacophonous. I listened for several minutes as he immersed himself in his music. Deciding that he was determined to play until things changed, I opted to take a walk before dinner. I asked Holmes if he cared to join me, but received only a grunt for my answer.

It was a lovely afternoon, and after a leisurely stroll, I soon found myself at the Avenue Gardens in Regent's Park, which some have called the Italian Gardens. I was struck by the order that man had imposed on nature, and as I thought about it, my mind turned to Holmes. It suddenly occurred to me that he was engaged in a similar quest: To bring order to a chaotic world.

Given that new perspective, I spent a few additional moments looking at the works with new eyes and appreciation. Had I known what lie ahead, I suspect I might have lingered there a while longer.

As I turned to begin my journey home, a youngster ran up to me and said, "Doctor, Mister 'Olmes needs you now."

Chapter 16

When I entered the sitting room, Holmes was pacing in front of his chair. He was much different from when I had left him. However, he jumped up at my arrival, and said, "Finally! I was torn between searching for you and sitting here awaiting your return. So I dispatched the Irregulars with orders to find you."

"Yes, one of them approached me in the park. I can only assume you've had some urgent news from Madame Pittorino?"

"Not as yet," he replied.

"Then what, pray tell, has happened?"

"This arrived about fifteen minutes after you departed." With that Holmes handed me a telegram.

> *"Your actions place not only yourself but others in jeopardy as well. This is your final warning Mr. Holmes."*

"My word, this is outrageous, Holmes. This cannot stand!"

"It shall not. I have already advised Mrs. Hudson that she might want to visit her relatives. Of course, she steadfastly refused, so I am going to ask Lestrade to have a constable keep a close eye on her. As for Mycroft, I have sent a message to him as well."

"To what end?"

"Whoever is behind this knows that I will not be put off by threats. I think he or she is counting on my fondness for those few individuals that I hold dear to dissuade me from pursuing this investigation any further."

"Holmes, you said 'he or she.' Surely, you can't imagine a woman could be behind this."

"And why not. Consider The Forty Thieves – the all-female gang that is the scourge of honest businessmen in the Elephant and Castle District. Some of the members are far more ruthless than any man."

I thought of my friend, Carlyle, who had opened an emporium in the West End and lost so much money to shoplifters and thieves in his first year that he had relocated to Cambridge in hopes of improving his fortunes. "Yes, I suppose you are right."

I then returned the conversation to the present predicament. "You know, Holmes, between the Alfred Jewel and the Founders Jewel and your obvious knowledge of the different techniques employed in the construction of such baubles, perhaps you should add consulting medievalist to your other credits and broker the deals for the museums yourself. That way you can make certain anything they bid on is genuine. That would certainly reduce the number of counterfeits being purchased."

He merely smiled at me and said, "Perhaps, I shall, Watson. Perhaps I shall."

At dinner Holmes was more reticent than usual, and my few attempts at conversation were rebuffed.

It was only after we had enjoyed a smoke and the page had knocked on the door with a letter for Holmes that I saw his eyes glisten and his entire demeanour change.

After he had read the letter twice and sat back in his chair, I was faced with a conundrum. I feared disturbing his train of thought but at the same time, I was eager to learn what the letter said that had caused such a sea change in my friend.

As I sat there trying to decide which course to pursue, Holmes suddenly interrupted my reverie. "The letter is from Madame Pittorino, and she says that she would be happy to assist in any way possible – within reason."

"Well that should come as good news?"

"It is not totally unexpected. These counterfeits undermine her business as well, so it is in her own interests to staunch the flow of bogus goods."

As he said that, he stopped, looked at me and said, "That's it."

"What's it, Holmes?"

"The solution to our problem. You provided half of it earlier and now Madame Pittorino has provided the rest. It simply falls to me to figure out how to marry the two and turn them to our advantage. And I have an idea how I might begin putting the pieces into place."

With that, he stepped into his bedroom, and unless I had seen Holmes go in, I should have never recognized the personage that emerged some thirty minutes later as my friend. "My word," I exclaimed, "I don't think your own brother would recognize you."

"That's precisely the point," he replied as he adjusted his helmet.

There standing before me was one of the fiercest looking constables I had ever seen. He seemed even taller than Holmes and my friend's thin frame appeared to have added several stone. The *piece de resistance* consisted of a luxurious red beard augmented by an equally extravagant pair of mutton chops that cleverly concealed most of his visage. However, anyone seeing him on the street could not help but notice the facial accoutrements and this constable could never been mistaken for the lean, ascetic-looking Holmes.

"Hiding in plain sight?" I said.

"Exactly," he replied. "Our adversary would also have to be boldness personified were he to assault a representative of the law."

"And such a formidable one at that."

"I will slip out the back entrance. I may be gone for several hours, Watson, so while there's no need to wait up, I would ask you to remain indoors and away from the windows. I shall impart the same instructions to Mrs. Hudson."

I yelled "Good luck, Holmes," as I heard him descending the stairs.

As he had promised, Holmes did not return until long after I had fallen asleep even though I had kept vigil for him until midnight. Still, when I made my way downstairs for breakfast the next morning, he was sitting at the table, reading the paper and enjoying a cup of coffee.

"I didn't hear you come in," I said. "I hope, given the late hour that you had a productive evening."

"Indeed, things could not have gone any better had I arranged them myself."

"So is there light at the end of this tunnel?"

"I can definitely discern illumination in the distance. Do you mean to say its presence eludes you?"

"Dash it all, Holmes, no one can keep up with you. So would you care to point us poor benighted souls in the direction of the light?"

"If you mean, will I explain everything that you have seen but failed to appreciate? If that is your question, the answer is a resounding 'No!' However, if you seek but a general sense of direction, I would suggest there are two distinct threads running throughout this case, and if you are to arrive at the same conclusion as I, you must look for the points where they converge. The happy confluence, as it were."

Of course, I had no idea about any threads running through the case – much less two that apparently converged at several points. As I started to eat, Holmes said, "I see you are serving as a locum today. Will you be free this evening?"

I had no idea how Holmes had ascertained that fact, but since he was unwilling to share his insights, I decided not to provide him with the praise for his deductive skills that he so enjoyed.

"Indeed, I am filling in for Dr. Cane, and yes, as of now, I am free this evening."

So I ate in silence while Holmes continued reading the paper. Finally, after I had enjoyed a second cup of coffee, I glanced at my watch and saw that I would be just on time. I said to Holmes, "I will see you for dinner." I then walked across the room, donned my coat and picked up my bag which I always leave by the door. However, as I opened the portal, I heard Holmes exclaim, "Aren't you forgetting something?"

"I don't think so," I replied rather testily. "Why? What is it that you think I am leaving behind?"

""It's not that you are leaving something behind, it's that you should leave something behind."

"I really don't have time for more riddles, Holmes."

"Well, if you want to treat patients with a napkin tucked into your shirt, who am I to dissuade you?"

Looking down, I saw the offending piece of linen still covering my shirt. Despite my irritation, I had to laugh in spite of myself.

"Now, Watson. You do deserve better, so I will provide you with a something to ponder during your free time. Will that suffice?"

"That would be greatly appreciated," I replied.

"Consider then: What might someone do with a copy of an artifact such as the Mérode Cup – a copy so perfect that it could deceive the top experts in the field? When you have arrived at a solution, then we shall take the next step together."

All the while he had been talking, Holmes had been donning his coat and filling his pockets with an array of items. "I will see you out, old friend, and then our directions will diverge. As you might expect, I have a great many things to which I must attend with regard to the upcoming festivities."

By this time, we had reached the street. I hailed a cab, but Holmes headed in the opposite direction on foot along Park Road in the general direction of St. James Wood.

In the cab, I pondered his question about the Mérode Cup, which seemed to have been the origin for this adventure. As I tossed over his words, I was suddenly struck by his parting remark, and I asked myself: "What 'upcoming festivities' was he talking about?"

Chapter 17

When I returned to Baker Street for lunch, I found another note waiting for me from Holmes:

If possible, meet me at Madame Pittorino's

at 5 p.m. If impossible, make every effort

to meet me there anyway.

S.H.

Although I had a busy afternoon, I cancelled my last patient, an elderly hypochondriac plagued by what he believed to be a chronic case of gout, and hailed a cab at precisely half four. Some twenty-eight minutes later, I alighted in front of the antique shop. The door was locked, but I rapped rather loudly, and a minute or so later, the clerk, whom I had met on our first visit, opened the door, just as Big Ben began to strike the hour in the distance.

"Well, aren't you the punctual one?" she laughed. "They are waiting for you in the back."

I made my way to Madame Pittorino's office to find that she and Holmes and were deep in conversation. As I entered, Holmes rose and greeted me, "Right on time. I have been making plans with Madame Pittorino, and she has agreed to help in my little conspiracy.

"While we are in agreement about almost all aspects of the plan, we find ourselves at odds as to which of the festivities should occur first."

"You keep mentioning 'festivities,' Holmes. I hope you realize that I have no idea about any upcoming galas, soirees or any other forms of entertainment."

"My apologies, old friend. I sometimes get ahead of myself and inevitably believe that everyone else is seeing things just as I am."

Madame Pittorino said, "After just two visits, I am reasonably certain that no one sees things quite as you do, Mr. Holmes."

I nodded at her and said, "Thank you Madame. I have been trying to tell him that exact same thing for years but to no avail."

"At any rate," Holmes continued, "we are planning two events. One will be an auction such as we attended the other evening."

"And what, pray tell, will you be auctioning off?"

At my question, Madam Pittorino opened an ornate wooden box which had been sitting on her desk. Reaching inside, she withdrew two small items and handed them to me. "Why these look like tiny knights carved out of ivory," I exclaimed.

"You are partially correct, Doctor," Madame Pittorino said, "They are two pieces, pawns to be precise, from a Scottish chess set known as the Lewis or Ulg chessmen. They date from the 12th century but were discovered only in 1831. All told, pieces from four different sets were found on the Isle of Lewis, hence the name. Carved from walrus tusk, these two were part of the so-called 'Lewis hoard.'"

"My word," I exclaimed examining them more closely, "they are exquisite." As I held them up, I marveled at the figures' clothing and gestures and wondered what historians had been able to glean about medieval society from their discovery.

"It is rather apropos, don't you think?" asked Holmes.

"What is?" I asked.

"Using pawns from a chess set as part of our gambit to bring a ring of murderers and counterfeiters to justice."

"Holmes, I can't say that I ever would have made that association, but now that you mention it, it certainly does seem appropriate."

"I must congratulate you on your *mot juste,* Mr. Holmes," added Madam Pittorino.

"And what of the other 'festivity' you mentioned?"

"That will be a legitimate auction to see which museum is most intent on acquiring the Alfred Jewel."

"I see, so whoever bids on both pieces will obviously be our criminal."

"It's not that simple, old friend. To begin with, I imagine there will be several people actively bidding on both pieces. Also, the criminal may send a surrogate or surrogates to bid in his or her stead. Would that it were that simple."

"Well, then what is the point of these auctions if not to draw the criminal out?"

Holmes then explained exactly how the plan would progress, following the bidding. After he had finished, he added,

"So that is why we were discussing which to hold first. There are advantages to be gleaned from holding either one first, it just remains to consider the merits of both arguments on balance. As you may have surmised, this could lead to a somewhat more drawn-out process than I would like, and I am trying to ascertain if there is any way to expedite matters and at the same time increase the odds of success."

"We are dealing with murderers and thieves, Holmes. I should think care – both for those involved as well as the items – should be our foremost concern."

"Of course, you are correct, Watson. As you know, I have been threatened; therefore, I have taken certain precautions. Madame Pittorino, I want to make you aware of the very real danger that exists."

"I am not a brave woman, Mr. Holmes, nor am I a foolish one. Every time I make a purchase or travel abroad, there is a certain element of risk. All we can do is try to minimize the danger and carry on. I refuse to live in fear."

"Still, I could have an extra constable assigned to this street," offered Holmes.

"That might scare off some of my regulars," she laughed, and the tension was suddenly broken. "Now then, where were we?"

"I believe we were discussing the order of events," replied my friend, and they resumed their discussion to which I contributed little but learned a great deal. After another forty-five minutes, plans had been tentatively finalized. As you can imagine there were a number of elements that had to be considered and people to be approached before anything could be set in stone.

After we had left Madame Pittorino and begun looking for a cab, Holmes said, "I took the liberty of telling Mrs. Hudson that we would not be home in time for dinner. So what do you fancy, old man?"

We decided to dine at Rules, one of London's oldest – and foremost – establishments. Holmes opted for the salmon with capers while I chose the Gressingham duck breast with runner beans. It was a delightful evening and as we sat there savoring an after-dinner port, one of Holmes' street urchins appeared at our table.

Before the lad could speak, a waiter appeared and grabbed the youngster by his shirt collar. Turning to Holmes, he said, "I apologize Mr. Holmes. I have no idea how this rascal gained entrance, but he won't be bothering you any longer." With that he started to drag the youngster, who was yelling and battling in an effort to free himself, towards the front door.

"Hold there," said Holmes. He then threw some money on the table and freed the boy from the waiter's grasp. "We were just leaving," he threw over his shoulder.

Outside, he looked at the boy, "Henry, what has happened?"

"They got 'em, Mister 'Olmes. They got Davey and Larry."

"Who's got them?" asked my friend.

"I don't know," replied the boy. "Two men came and grabbed them and threw them in a cab. They said, 'Tell 'Olmes this is what happens when 'e ignores warnings."

"I never thought they would threaten children, Watson. We must act and act quickly."

Turning back to the youngster, Holmes asked, "Where were you when the boys were grabbed?"

"We were standing on the corner of Alie Street and Leman Street when this cab pulled up. Two men jumped out and said 'Mister 'Olmes sent us. 'E needs two volunteers – double the usual rate.' I thought I'd get picked for sure, but 'e chose Davey and Larry – the two youngest."

"Yes, and the two easiest to control," I offered.

"Which way did the cab go? Towards Spitalfields or towards the river?"

"Towards the river," replied the boy.

"One last question and think hard: Did you happen to notice the number on the cab?"

At that Henry finally found a smile, "Of course, sir, we are trained, y'know! Number 52!"

Holmes immediately hailed a hansom and we headed for Baker Street. During the ride, he asked the boy if he knew where Wiggins could be found.

The youngster said, "He usually runs a game of 'Find the Lady' down on the Embankment by Blackfriars Bridge." Holmes banged on the roof and told the driver our new destination. About a quarter of an hour later, we arrived. Upon descending, I spotted Wiggins and several of his mates. Holmes emitted a sharp whistle. Looking up and recognizing my friend, they stopped the game and ran to him

Holmes told them what had happened, "Wiggins, I need you and all the lads you know – not just the Irregulars — to find cab Number 52. Travel in groups of three and four. As soon as you locate it, get the driver's name and send him to Baker Street. If he will not come, send a messenger to Baker Street and fetch me. Time is of the essence, lads. And be careful!" With that Holmes handed Wiggins some notes. "And a £5 note to the boys who find the cab."

With that, they began to break up into small groups and scatter. In the cab back to Baker Street, Holmes spoke but once and that was more to himself than me: "I shall never forgive myself if anything should happen to those brave lads."

We kept a lonely vigil by the fire for the next few hours. Shortly after midnight, the bell rang. Holmes had advised Mrs. Hudson that we might be having late visitors and that stalwart lady had insisted upon staying up to answer the door herself.

A minute later, there was a knock on the door and Holmes opened it to see Wiggins standing there with a rather disheveled looking individual. "This 'ere is Mr. Joshua Carp, the owner of cab Number 52."

"Thank you, Wiggins. We will settle up tomorrow."

"But what about Davey and Larry?" Wiggins asked. "I want to 'elp."

"You have already provided invaluable assistance, and besides, I have another assignment for you tomorrow. Now get some sleep and call here at noon."

The look of disappointment on Wiggins' face was touching, but he snapped off a salute and said, "Yes, sir." Then he clattered down the stairs as he was wont to do and, surprisingly, closed the front door rather gently.

Turning to the driver, Holmes said, "Won't you come in, Mr. Carp?"

"I should be workin'," the man replied rather testily, "not here talkin' to the likes of you."

After Holmes said, "Not to worry. You will be compensated for your time," the man's demeanour changed completely.

"How may I be of service," said the man, trying to enunciate each word. The fact that he had been drinking would have been obvious to almost anyone.

"Earlier this evening, you picked up a fare on Leman Street – two men and two boys – do you recall?"

"Certainly! The men said the boys had run off from the parish workhouse and they were suspected of stealing several items. They said they were returning 'em to face justice."

"Just so," replied Holmes.

As if for emphasis, Carp added, "I tell ya, the youngsters put up a quite a fight, kicking and screaming and biting and such."

"Do you remember where you left them?" asked Holmes.

"I took them down to a warehouse on Thomas More Street, right where it runs into Burr Close, near St. Katharine's Docks."

"Didn't it strike you as odd that they took the boys to the docks rather than the workhouse?"

"It did," he replied, "but they said they was meeting several other people there."

At that Holmes smiled. "Mr. Carp, we shall be down momentarily."

"You mean you're 'iring' me?"

"Indeed," replied Holmes. As the man descended the stairs, Holmes turned to me and said, "I think your service sidearm would be a pleasant companion on this excursion." I nodded and went to my room to fetch it. When I returned, we headed downstairs. Holmes, I noticed, was carrying a heavy walking stick.

As we entered the cab, Carp called down, "Where to?"

"The warehouse on Thomas More Street but stop on the street before it."

As the horse clattered off, Holmes looked at me and said, "I pray we are not too late."

Chapter 18

After a short walk, we arrived at Thomas More Street. It was dark and deserted. Looking up at Carp, Holmes said, "Do you know which warehouse they went in?"

"Yes sir, the red one just a bit along there on the right,"

"Excellent, now I want you to go to the Bishopgate police station and tell the officer at the desk that Sherlock Holmes requests an inspector and two constables as soon as possible." Holmes then handed the man a few notes and he whipped up his horse, returning as we had come.

"Do you have a plan, Holmes?"

"Just a rudimentary one: Divide and conquer."

"How do you anticipate doing that?"

Holmes then explained what he had in mind. After he had finished, he said, "Wait five minutes. If I'm not back, you know what to do."

I must have checked my watch at least thirty times during the next five minutes. When Holmes did not return, I walked to the front door of the warehouse and knocked three times as loudly as I could. I then dashed across the street and hid behind some ashcans. I watched as a large man opened the door, He peered about and after seeing nothing, he returned to the inside of the warehouse, closing the door behind him.

I looked at my watch and let three more minutes pass, then I ran across the street and knocked on the door again. As soon as I had done so, I dashed back to my hiding place.

Once again, the door was opened by the same man. This time, however, he peered into the alley next to the warehouse using a dark lantern to illuminate the passage. Finally, he yelled, "If I catch you, you'll be sorry."

After he had finished searching and yelling, he went back inside. I knew this next part was the most dangerous, for he was alert and no doubt expecting another prank. So I carried a cover for an ashcan with me and after the first knock, I threw it into the alley where it landed with a clatter while I dashed five feet to the left and flattened myself against the wall. The door opened almost immediately, and had I tried to run back across the street, he would have almost certainly seen me.

However, my distraction had the desired effect, as he turned towards the alley. He entered about three feet and stood there peering into the darkness, aided by his lantern. I crept up behind him, put my revolver to the base of his neck and said quietly, but firmly, "Do not move or make a sound." I pushed him against the wall, and handcuffed him with a pair of darbies which Holmes had provided.

"How many others are inside?"

Before he could answer, I heard a sharp whistle and then another – Holmes' signal that everything was under control.

I marched my prisoner inside where I found another man, sitting on the floor, his hands secured behind his back. He had obviously suffered a blow to the head as his scalp was matted with blood. I placed my prisoner on the floor so that they were sitting back-to-back.

Holmes was busily untying the boys who appeared unharmed.

After their gags had been removed, they both thanked Holmes for saving them. Turning back to our prisoners, Holmes said, "You have one chance to help yourselves. Tell us who hired you, and I shall put in a good word with Scotland Yard. Refuse, and I shall do everything in my power to see that you spend the rest of your wretched lives in jail.

"Don't try to look at each other," Holmes cautioned. Then he glanced at me, and said, "Watson, how long before the police arrive?"

"They should be here any minute."

"Your time is running short. Last chance," he cautioned them.

Suddenly, the one I had captured said, "It was a fellow named Roberts. We wasn't going to hurt the lads. We just took them to scare you."

"What did this Roberts say?"

At that point, the man Holmes had hit yelled, "Shut up, Bill. I'd rather face justice than Roberts and the boss."

"The boss?" enquired Holmes. "Bill, do you have any idea who that might be?"

"No sir, I never met the boss – only Roberts and Sam here."

"Shut up, Bill, before it's too late," Sam threatened.

"We was told to grab these two boys and hold 'em until we heard from Roberts," Bill continued, paying no heed to the string of vulgar threats issuing from Sam's mouth.

At that point, there was a clatter of hooves in the street. "That would be the police," said Holmes. "Do make them aware of our presence, Watson."

I went to the door where I was greeted by Inspector Athelney Jones and two burly constables. I led them to Holmes.

"Well, this is a surprise, Mr. Holmes," exclaimed Jones. "What have we here?"

After recapping the evening's events, Holmes pulled Jones aside and said, "It is imperative that the men be kept apart as I fear one might try to do the other harm."

"What do you suggest, Mr. Holmes?"

"Take them to two different police stations, but make certain that Sam – the one on the right," Holmes said indicating our prisoners, "has no idea where his friend is being held. You can send a message to me at Baker Street, informing me of the particulars. Watson, would you be kind enough to escort the boys home?"

"Certainly, old man, but what will you be doing?"

"I want to examine these rooms a bit more carefully, so if you should encounter another cab en route, please send it here as I don't fancy a five-mile walk at this time of night."

As luck would have it, we passed a public house at the corner of Old Street with a cab lingering outside. I went inside, found the driver and told him where he might find Holmes.

"How do I know this ain't a wild goose chase?"

I tore a £5 note in half and gave him one portion. "The rest is yours when you have delivered Mr. Holmes to Baker Street."

"Wait! Am I pickin' up Sherlock Holmes?"

"Yes, now be quick about it."

"Why didn't you say that to begin with?" With that he practically sprinted out the door and his cab was at the end of the street when I emerged from the tavern.

About an hour later, I heard the front door open and I recognized my old friend's familiar tread as he ascended the stairs.

"Well, did you discover anything at the warehouse?"

"That remains to be seen," replied Holmes rather evasively.

"That means that something has struck you. What else was inside?"

"There were various crates – some filled with machinery while several others contained china. They were clearly marked for export. While the rest of the room was filled with crates of pottery as well as casks of wine and olive oil. Finally, there were also sacks of rice, tea and guano from Peru present. The latter with its particularly pungent odor was the least enjoyable part of my explorations."

"Yes, but did the warehouse yield any clues?"

"Of that I am not yet certain; however, I may be able to tell a great deal more tomorrow after I have corresponded with Mycroft. Now, old friend, it has been a long day and tomorrow promises more of the same." With that Holmes headed for his bedroom, and after extinguishing the lamp, I climbed the stairs to my own room.

I must have been more tired than I thought, for I slept quite soundly and didn't awaken until half eight.

I expected to see Holmes at breakfast but Mrs. Hudson informed me he had risen early, had only a cup of coffee and then departed.

Since I had a number of patients to see – the first one scheduled for eleven o'clock – I suspected that I probably wouldn't learn any more from Holmes until dinner that evening – if then.

My day seemed interminable, and it was made longer by two emergencies in the afternoon. When the last patient had departed shortly before five, I quickly closed my surgery. As the sky was threatening, I decided to hail a cab and treat myself to a carriage ride home.

I ascended the stairs and found Holmes sitting at his chemistry table. "Ah, Watson, you have had a busy day, I see."

"No parlor tricks today, Holmes. What did you learn about the warehouse?"

"The warehouse is owned by the Worldwide Trading Company."

"Well that would explain the imports and exports, I suppose."

"Indeed, but I'm more interested in the imports at present."

"To what end?"

"Consider the source," he said enigmatically.

He then pulled a letter from his breast pocket. "I have heard from Madame Pittorino, and our next clandestine auction is scheduled for Friday evening – the day after the museum auction."

"I suppose there is a point to having the museum go first?"

"I should think the order would be rather obvious by now."

Not wishing to appear totally in the dark, I held my tongue, vowing that I would elicit the information from Holmes on another occasion.

"The museum auction will be held in the old Bonham's sale room at the Montpelier Galleries in Montpelier Street. There will only be a few people present. Obviously, representatives from the British and the South Kensington Street Museums will be in attendance as well as notables from National Museum of Denmark, the National Museum of Ireland and quite possibly the *Germanisches Nationalmuseum*." Holmes pronounced the latter in what I can only assume was flawless German."

"Given all those dignitaries, where will you and I fit in?"

"Look in the mirror, old friend, and tell me what you see?"

"I see myself, of course."

"Well, with a little makeup, I see Lord Thomas Chadwick, representing the Fitzwilliam Museum of Cambridge University."

"You cannot be serious."

"Ah, but I am. Furthermore I see the man who is going to outbid everyone else at the auction and secure the Alfred Jewel for the Fitzwilliam."

"And while I am making a fool of myself, trying to be something I am not, what will you be doing?"

"First of all, you give yourself far too little credit, old friend. Though you may not have a title, you have more innate nobility than many who claim that right based on their ancestors' achievements rather than their own actions. I have long discerned a certain *noblesse oblige* about your character which I have always admired."

I could feel my face flushing at these unexpected compliments, so I repeated the question to change the subject, "And again I ask: Where will you be?"

"I shall be around," was the only answer I could elicit from him.

The rest of the week passed with me preparing for the auction and trying to learn as much about medieval jewelry as I could.

When Friday arrived. Holmes had me sit in front of him as he applied a generous helping of spirit gum which was followed by a full beard and side-whiskers of a shade much darker than my own, He stepped back and studied his work. "Something distinctive is needed," he said. "Something obvious to set you apart." Holmes mixed up something that I could not see and then applied a thin line of the substance above my right eye. As he was standing between me and the mirror, I found it impossible to follow his actions. I just know that there was lots of dabbing and gentle rubbing. After about 10 minutes, he stood back, admired his work and said simply "Fencing accident, if anyone should ask."

When he finally stepped aside, I saw an evil scar traversing my forehead above my right eye. "Holmes, that is amazing," I exclaimed.

"And one more thing – your voice. Your natural timbre is rather distinctive, my friend. Rather than affect an accent that may betray you, try speaking in a much quieter tone than you normally do and don't open your mouth as wide. Try it."

I followed his directions and said, "I feel the fool. And now I'm mumbling as well." Still, I had to admit, I sounded nothing like my normal self.

"Keep practicing," said Holmes. "The important thing to remember is to stay in character. You must not slip or there could be dire consequences."

"I won't let you down," I promised, remembering to speak quietly with a semi-closed mouth.

"Excellent, old man. I knew I could depend on you. Now, go get dressed. I will meet you at the auction. A cab will be here for you at eight. I will be there when you arrive, but don't look for me.

"And remember, your purse is bottomless. No matter how high the bidding goes, you must emerge victorious.

"Now there is one more bit of business that you must handle for me." Holmes then told me exactly what to do when the auction was over. I must say after hearing his instructions, I was rather looking forward to the rest of the evening – as well as the following night.

Chapter 19

At exactly eight o'clock, I descended the stairs and stepped outside to find a fine carriage with two black stallions waiting for me. I stepped inside and the driver immediately whipped up the horses as we headed towards Bonhams.

Having been founded in 1793, it was just a few decades younger than both Christie's and Southeby's, but its reputation was on a par with those two esteemed auction houses. Some fifteen minutes later the carriage stopped in front of the auction room on Montpelier Street in Knightsbridge. I entered the showroom and saw a number of familiar faces, including Lawrence Burkhardt from the British Museum as well as all the members of the acquisitions committee, save Mycroft, from the South Kensington Museum. There were a number of people whom I did not recognize, but I did spy Mr. Lasalandra as well as Madame Pittorino among the others.

They all seemed to know each other, and I was definitely the outlier. Happily no one approached me and while champagne was available, I made the decision to abstain.

At exactly half eight, a bell tinkled and a sonorous voice announced, "Ladies and gentlemen, if you would kindly be seated." We were ushered into the backroom where rows of chairs had been set up and a small podium stood at the front next to a table. By now I was looking everywhere for Holmes, but he was nowhere to be seen.

My thoughts were interrupted by the auctioneer who said, "We have but five items on the block tonight, but they are all exquisite pieces, and our final offering is something quite special."

The first item was a sketch of Erasmus by Hans Holbein the Younger. The bidding was quite spirited, and as you might expect the representative of the *Germanisches Nationalmuseum* eventually emerged victorious. The second item was a Frankish brooch in the shape of a bird that Lawrence Burkhardt secured for the British Museum. The third item, an English anelace, or long dagger, was hotly contested but the South Kensington Museum managed to outbid everyone else for the right to exhibit it. The fourth item, a beautifully illustrated folio from a Book of Hours also elicited some spirited bidding, and surprisingly, Mr. Lasalandra submitted the high bid.

By this time, I noticed one or two of the other bidders glancing at me as I had yet to make a bid on any of the previous items.

"Our final item is one with which I am certain you are all familiar. Oxford University has decided to find a new home for the Alfred Jewel." With that, he held up a small rosewood box and opened the top to display it. "Those of you who wish may come up for a closer look and we shall begin the bidding in five minutes."

As the others crowded the stage for a closer look, I remained in my seat, trying to take in everything that was going on around me. After exactly five minutes, the auctioneer hit the table with his gavel and said, "Let us begin the bidding at £5,000. That was immediately answered, and the bidding was soon increasing in £100 increments. When the asking price hit £8,000, and the bidding slowed, I raised my hand to indicate I was willing to pay £8,100. That brought looks of consternation from both Burkhardt and the Kensington contingent, who had placed the bid previous to mine.

After a brief consultation, the Kensington group bid £8,200. We went back and forth a few more times, but my bid of £8,800 proved too much for them.

"Sold to Lord Thomas Chadwick, representing the Fitzwilliam Museum of Cambridge University," intoned the auctioneer.

I lingered allowing the others to secure their purchases and commiserate or congratulate. Finally, I approached the podium. After handing the auctioneer the letter of credit which Holmes had entrusted to me, he examined it and handed me the box, saying, "Congratulations, Your Lordship. I am so happy the Alfred Jewel is remaining here in England."

"Thank you," I replied.

"Would you like us to hold it here or will you be taking it with you."

"If you would hail me a cab, I shall take it with me and put it in the safe at the Northumberland Hotel."

A minute later, the auctioneer returned, "Your cab is waiting, Lord Chadwick."

I was still casting about for Holmes. I even examined the driver more closely than I might have before I climbed into the cab. Although the face looked vaguely familiar, I was certain it wasn't Holmes.

As the auctioneer closed the cab door, the last thing he said to me was "Well done, Watson."

As you might expect I was stunned to hear my friend's voice when I least expected it, but I was glad he had been there to witness everything that had transpired.

After a ride of some twenty minutes, I found myself exiting the cab in front of the hotel. I gave my assumed name to a disinterested desk clerk, whose demeanour changed immediately upon hearing it, and was escorted to a suite on the third floor. "Your luggage arrived earlier, Lord Chadwick," a bellhop informed me.

The room was spacious, although I must admit I was hoping for the Savoy or the Metropole when Holmes informed me that I would be staying at a hotel. A few minutes later, there was a gentle knock on the door and a voice said, "Room Service."

I cautiously opened the door and the bellboy reappeared with a tray bearing glasses, a gasogene and bottles of whisky and brandy. "Compliments of the management, sir." I slipped him a few coins and he departed.

After pouring myself a whisky and soda, I heard someone fiddling with the lock on the door. I retrieved my Webley just as I heard Holmes say, "Don't shoot, old man."

I breathed a sigh of relief and, after stashing the Webley in my pocket, said, "Care to join me?"

After I had made Holmes a drink, he said, "That went about as well as could be expected."

"Did it?"

"You couldn't see what I saw from the stage, Watson. There was a great deal of acrimony among the members of the Kensington Street Museum delegation – especially with regards to bidding on the Alfred Jewel."

"They did put up quite a fight."

"Yes, and if one or two others had got their way, we might still be bidding."

We then discussed our plans for the following evening. "I expect that it will be similar in many ways to the last such auction we attended," Holmes said.

"I should hope so as that was a rather enjoyable evening."

"We can only hope that the rancor that some of these collectors feel for each other does not raise its ugly head."

"These are all well-born, influential people, I would hardly expect any bitterness to be made manifest."

"No, I suppose you are right, old friend." With that Holmes finished his drink and said, "I shall see you tonight at eight to help with your facial accoutrements."

I winced at the thought.

Holmes seeing my obvious displeasure said, "You must soldier on for one more night." Then knowing how to appeal to my better side, he added, "For Queen and Country."

I remember thinking, "Blast you, Holmes," but I knew – as did he – that there was no way I would shirk my duty. As he reached the door, I stood and repeated, "For Queen and Country."

The next day seemed an eternity. Having checked in wearing my disguise, I was loath to leave my room without it. As a result, I spent much of the day reading and organizing my notes on a previous case. I was pleasantly surprised when

Holmes arrived around six and we enjoyed a leisurely supper together – or should I say I enjoyed. As was his wont when he was involved in a case, my friend barely touched his food.

After we had enjoyed a brandy and a cigar, he looked at his watch, smiled mischievously and said simply, "It's time."

From a satchel he retrieved all the items he had used on me the previous evening and reattached the whiskers and the scar. After he had finished, he stepped back and appraised me with a critical eye. Finally, he smiled and said, "Just remember to modulate your voice."

Suddenly it hit me. "Holmes, if this is going to be like the last auction we attended and everyone will be masked, why do I need all these theatrics?"

"Simple, dear Doctor. When you come up at the end of the auction to take possession of the pawns from the Lewis hoard, I want you to allow your mask to slip."

"What on Earth for?"

"Quite simple: I want everyone who attends to know who will be taking those chess pieces home."

"You're baiting a trap."

"One might say that," he replied.

"And I am the cheese."

"Not exactly, the pawns are the cheese, you are merely the conveyer of the cheese."

"Well, I must admit, knowing that makes me feel a great deal better."

Looking at me earnestly, Holmes said, "There is no one else I would rather have carry out this mission than you, old friend. I need a cool head and a steady hand if it comes to that. And personal experience has shown me that you possess both."

With that we headed for the door, and upon reaching it, he handed me a raven's feather and said, "Don't forget this, you will need it." I placed it in my inside jacket pocket.

"I will see you there. I expect far fewer people this time, so you may be under greater scrutiny than previously." As he turned to leave, he gave me a final once-over and then said, "One more thing – it's evening dress – and for you that now includes your pistol." With that final remark, he strode down the hall towards the stairs.

At exactly half nine, I left the hotel and once again there was a carriage waiting for me. Truth be told, it might have been the exact same Clarence that had conveyed Holmes and me to the previous auction. As I expected, the curtains had been drawn and secured so that I would have no idea where I was being taken – had I not made the trip previously.

I was quite surprised when some twenty minutes later, the cab stopped. After donning my mask and alighting from the Clarence, I found myself standing in front of an entirely different warehouse. I could only hope Holmes was aware of the change of venue.

Standing in front of the entrance was a burly doorman. However, when I produced my feather, he smiled, opened the door for me and said, "Have a good evening, sir."

I entered the warehouse and was surprised to find myself in an ornately decorated room. Waiters were passing through the crowd of some thirty people or so, passing out champagne and taking orders for those who wanted something stronger.

Taking stock of the situation, I began to see whom I might recognize – despite the masks. There was a petite woman in an electric blue gown that I suspected might be Madame Pittorino but the mask was different from the one she had worn previously. As I was lost in thought, I was gently jostled by another man. As he apologized, I took his measure and after noticing his tiepin and cufflinks decided that Mr. Lasalandra was also present.

Again, no one tried to start a conversation with me, and I was just as glad that I was allowed to remain aloof. At exactly ten, one of the waiters asked us to take our seats. I followed the crowd into a smaller room where chairs had been set up and sat myself at the end of the last row.

As I have indicated, this was, for lack of a better term, an illicit auction, so I do hope you will understand if I refrain from naming the items that were bid on. Suffice to say a number were well-known works of art such as might be seen in the grand country estates of our nobility.

The bidding was fierce for several pieces, including one painting which I am certain would be familiar to the vast majority of my readers. In fact, on that one occasion two of the bidders nearly came to blows.

Finally, the auctioneer, a short, bald man with just a hint of a French accent, announced the evening's final lot. "To bring things to a conclusion, we have two pawns from the Lewis chessmen. Dating from the twelfth century, these exquisite pieces were carved from walrus ivory and discovered in 1831 on the island of Lewis in the Outer Hebrides.

"As they are quite small, I will allow those interested to examine them before the auction commences."

Perhaps four or five people went up to get a closer look at the chessmen while I remained in my seat.

After everyone had retaken their seats, the auctioneer said, "Do I have an opening bid of £3,000?"

A woman in the front row opened the bidding, and in no time we were at £5,000. "Do I hear £5,100? £5,100 anyone?" At that point I made my first bid. In less than a minute, we were at £5,500. The auctioneer asked, "Do I hear £5,600?"

Deciding to end it – after all, it wasn't my money – I jumped to £6,000. The auctioneer tried to work the room, but there were no takers. "£6,000, going once, £6,000, going twice. Sold for £6,000 to the man in the last row.

"Thank you ladies and gentlemen. Our business this evening is concluded. Hopefully, we will be gathering again in the very near future."

I waited until the crowd had thinned before I approached the stage. I produced the letter of credit, which I then gave to the auctioneer. After examining it, he handed me a beautiful ebony box. Opening it, I saw the two chessmen resting on a cushion of green velvet. Moving to the side of the room, where the light was better, I turned my back to those remaining and lifted my mask in order to examine the pieces. I then asked the auctioneer if I might borrow a glass. Pulling a lens such as Holmes often used from his pocket, he handed it to me. I then inspected the pawns quite carefully. As you might suspect, it was all a show for those present.

Following that I produced a jeweler's loupe which Holmes had provided and examined the pieces even more circumspectly.

The auctioneer looked on as I conducted my examination. At one point, he remarked, "Aren't you the cautious one? I can assure you, sir, that all the articles are genuine. We have no truck with forgers. They are a blight on the business."

As he was speaking, I issued a series of utterances and compliments, such as "Magnificent!" and "Exquisite!" I then turned back to the auctioneer to return the lens, deliberately forgetting to remove the loupe and replace my mask. In the distance, I heard someone whisper, "That's Lord Chadwick."

Then as if suddenly becoming aware of my *faux pas*, I quickly lowered my mask, returned the glass and asked one of the waiters to hail me a cab as I wished to go to the Northumberland Hotel.

The ride back was uneventful, and I ascended to my room without incident. I was uncertain whether I should remove my beard and side-whiskers, so I decided to wait until I heard from Holmes.

As I sat there smoking, I noticed a bottle sitting atop the chest of drawers. It was a bottle of Armagnoc and attached to it was a note that simply said, "A bravura performance!" Even in just those few words, I thought I recognized Holmes' rather spidery hand. Deciding I had earned a nightcap, I opened it and poured a healthy glass. As I sat there enjoying the rather fine brandy, I took a good look at myself in the mirror. I was thinking that the facial hair imbued me with a certain gravitas that might be found lacking in my everyday appearance.

I was stirred from my thoughts by a gentle tapping at the connecting door to the next room. The rapping was repeated. Drawing my pistol, I went to the door. "Who's there?"

"A friend, Watson."

Recognizing Holmes' voice, I threw open the door and found myself staring at my own reflection in a full-length mirror.

Chapter 20

As you might expect, I was dumfounded. Before I could say anything, the image spoke, "Aren't you going to invite me in, old man? I could use a drink myself."

"Holmes, what does this mean? Why are you dressed and made up to look like me?"

"You are – or should I say, I am – expecting a visitor. This must be handled with a great deal of care. We have led them to our trap, now we must slowly begin to close it. I know precisely how I want this to play out, but I have no idea how they will react, so if you are not too offended, I will take your place for the rest of the evening."

"But Holmes, why send me to the auction in disguise when you could have gone yourself?"

Before he could answer, there was a gentle rapping at the door. "Lord Chadwick, I am sorry to disturb you so late, but it is a matter of some importance. The hotel manager informed me that you had returned to your room about thirty minutes ago."

Holmes raised a finger to his lips and then ushered me toward the connecting door. "Leave it slightly ajar and listen carefully," he mouthed. Then in an uncanny imitation of the voice I had been using, he mumbled rather softly. "Just give me a moment, please."

I watched through the narrow slit as Holmes checked his appearance in the mirror and then with a slightly stooped posture, he turned toward the door.

"Who is it?" he asked.

"My name is John Roberts, and I have a proposition which I believe you will find exceedingly interesting – and quite profitable."

Out of sight, I heard Holmes open the door. "It is nearly midnight, sir. I sincerely hope this matter is urgent."

"I think you will be glad you decided to listen to me, Your Lordship."

I saw in the mirror, Holmes invite Roberts in, then he said, "Get to it! I am a busy man."

"Let me begin by congratulating you on securing both the Alfred Jewel and the Lewis chessmen for the museum at Cambridge."

"I assume you were at the auction tonight; otherwise, you could not have known."

"Actually, I was not, but my confederate was there, bidding against you, and he informed me of your victory."

"That's as may be," said Holmes. "You still haven't told me what you want."

"There are actually two things I want, and you may choose to accept either of my propositions – or both."

"Get on with it," Holmes muttered irritably.

"First, with regard to the Lewis chessmen, I am prepared to offer you £500 to give them to me."

Holmes laughed, "£500? I just paid £6,000 for them at the auction. Only a fool would accept that deal."

"You misunderstand me, sir. I will refund the £6,000 and another £500 for you to pocket. No one at Cambridge will ever know. All you have to do is tell them you were outbid. What was your limit, if I may ask?"

"I was prepared to go to £6,500."

"So you see, no one gets hurt and no one is the wiser, but you are the winner."

"Interesting," said Holmes, "and your other proposition."

"I will pay you another £500 if you will allow me to borrow the Alfred Jewel for two days."

"For what purpose? I am scheduled return to Cambridge tomorrow."

"Just wire them and say you were delayed by paperwork and such and you will be returning two days hence."

"What assurance do I have that once I give you the Alfred Jewel you will return it intact and unharmed."

"I give you my word as a gentleman."

"Sir, you are no gentleman – you are a thief and a scoundrel, so I am afraid your word will hardly suffice."

"Well, what else can I offer you?"

"Obviously, you have done this sort of thing before, so I would be willing to hold something of equal value. When you return the Alfred Jewel, I will return your item."

"I'm not certain ..."

"Sir, you are obviously a messenger – a mere minion as it were – and I do not deal with minions."

"Please understand, Lord Chadwick..."

"I understand that if I am to become involved in your enterprise, for lack of a better term, I am taking a serious risk. Now, tell your employer that he must take the same risk and meet me face to face if our business is to go forward. If the prospect of meeting me so unnerves him that he finds it intolerable, then he must seek out another partner.

"I will delay my return to Cambridge for two days. If I haven't heard from you within that time, I will consider our business to be at an end. You may see yourself out."

I waited in silence for several minutes. Finally Holmes rose, opened the door to the hall and after closing it, said, "The coast is clear, Watson."

"My word!" I exclaimed, "I'm not certain how I would have handled that."

"I'm positive you would have conducted yourself with an unparalleled degree of aplomb. However, I needed to drive home the message that I would not deal with underlings. I also didn't anticipate him asking to 'borrow' the Alfred Jewel."

"I must confess that request took me by surprise as well, but I think you handled it admirably."

"That remains to be seen," replied Holmes. "The important thing is one way or another, we will hear from the mastermind behind this plot."

"Yes, I should think you made that abundantly clear."

"You're certain Roberts was nowhere near you at the auction."

"I'm positive! I think I would recall the face of a man who bound me with my own braces."

"True enough," said Holmes.

"Until they do contact us, you must remain in this room. I have a number of things to which I must attend. It is imperative that you do not answer the door if Roberts should return in person. After all, these are very sharp and dangerous customers. Should you do something differently from me or if he should detect the slightly different timbre of your voice, he may well put two and two together and realize he has been deceived.

"Now, let us enjoy a glass of that Armagnoc, and then I must be on my way. The next few days promise to be very busy ones."

As we sat there, I saw a slight smile play across Holmes' face. Then he turned to me and said, "Where is the Alfred Jewel? I assume you have the chessmen."

"The Alfred Jewel is in the hotel safe, and I have the chessmen right here." Saying that, I pulled the small box from my pocket.

"Excellent. I want you to go down to the front desk right now and retrieve the Jewel. I shall wait here, and when I leave I will take both with me. When you return, I'll explain exactly what I want you to do."

I think the night desk was rather surprised at my request, but a few minutes later, I was back in my room and handed both the Jewel and the pawns to Holmes. I watched as he removed the last of his makeup. When he had finished, he turned to me and said, "Don't wait in this room, but rather conceal yourself in the adjoining room."

"You think Roberts will return?"

"Roberts and one or more of his thugs. If they see the connecting door locked from this side, they will think you have gone out. So I will lock this door after you and you must be certain you lock the door on your side. Have all your meals sent up and be very still. If you should hear anything, give this note to a maid or a bellhop."

I looked and the note simply said:

Contact Inspector Lestrade.
Tell him to come immediately to
Room 310, Northumberland Hotel.

"Take care of yourself, Watson. I will be in touch."

I decided to have another glass of Armagnoc and then I set about removing my makeup. I will never understand why Holmes seems to delight in dressing up, but there is no denying his skill.

The next morning I awoke, and I was ravenously hungry. Unfortunately, the maid didn't come to change the room until just after ten. I told her what I required, and explained I was not feeling well. I'm sure she must have thought something was amiss considering the size of my breakfast order, but she said not a word. I gave her a pound for her troubles, and she said she would make certain the staff attended to all my needs.

I had finished my breakfast and was enjoying a second cup of coffee when I thought I heard a noise in the next room. I crept to the door and placed my ear against it. There was definitely someone in my room. After a minute or two, I heard a few words, though it was difficult to discern exactly what was said through the double doors. However, when he spoke again, I could distinctly make out the words "somewhere" and "boxes" quite clearly.

After about fifteen minutes, the room became quiet, and while I was fairly certain they had departed, I refrained from entering the room. So I waited and when the maid came to remove my dishes, I asked her if she had made up the next room.

"No sir," she replied, "I think the gentleman in there is staying another night or two."

"Would you be so kind as to knock on the door and see if he requires anything? Towels? Soap?" As I said this I slipped her another pound. After she left, I listened carefully. I heard her knock and no one answered, so I assumed the coast was clear. I was about to enter my room when I recalled that Holmes had locked the door from that side.

As a result, I spent the rest of the afternoon reading the papers and trying to fit the pieces of this puzzle together.

It was just before six that I heard a staccato rap on my door. I knew immediately it was Holmes. I let him in and after he had settled himself in a chair, I related the day's goings-on. When I had finished, he said, "Well done, Watson. Now let me enter that room and then I shall admit you.

A minute or two later, Holmes opened the connecting door. "It seems as though Mr. Roberts did stop by," he said. "When I entered the room, I saw immediately that it had been thoroughly searched. The mattress was on the floor; the paintings had been removed from the wall; and the chest of drawers had been ransacked and all my clothing was on the floor.

"It's a good thing you don't wear monogrammed shirts, old man. That might have been difficult to explain."

Pointing to the desk, I saw an envelope propped against the lamp. Pointing to it, I said, "Holmes, they left a letter."

After he had opened it, I watched as he perused it several times. Finally, he looked at me and said, "This is pretty much what I expected."

After he handed it to me, I read:

> *Regent's Park Boathouse, 11 p.m.*
> *Nautilus Cup for Alfred Jewel.*
> *R*

"That will not do at all, Watson."

"What do you mean?"

"I rather suspect that Mr. Roberts and his cohorts would like to get Lord Chadwick alone at night in Regent's Park – far from any help – and relieve him of whatever valuables he may be carrying."

"So what will you do?"

"Absolutely nothing. We shall treat ourselves to a pleasant dinner as we wait to hear from those rascals. My guess is one way or another they will contact Lord Chadwick tomorrow. They have baited their hook. As Lord Chadwick, I nibbled at the bait. Now, they must figure out how to reel His Lordship in. At the same time, I shall be endeavoring to bring this matter to a close."

"The Nautilus Cup mentioned in the note – what is it?"

"It is a stunning piece. Created in Holland in the late sixteenth or early seventeenth century, the Nautilus Cup – and there are several – is a standing cup made from a single nautilus shell mounted on a silver pedestal. The front features a rather grotesque sea monster with an open mouth. Astride the monster is an infant Hercules with a serpent in one hand and a spear in the other."

"It sounds both beautiful and bizarre."

"Yes, as Dr. Johnson might have said, it is a perfect example of *concordia discors*. At any rate, it is immaterial because I know for a fact they do not possess it."

"How can you be so certain?"

"I have been checking up on the status of a number of rare *objects d'art*. After an attempt was made to purchase it, which was declined, an effort to burgle the owner's home was attempted. Since that time, it has resided safely in a bank vault in Amsterdam."

"My word, but you are thorough."

Doffing our disguises, Holmes and I left the hotel through the tradesmen's entrance and dined at a small bistro near St. Pancras Station. "Since there will be no one to meet with Roberts tonight, have you anticipated his next move?"

Holmes chuckled, "Come now, old man. You know me better than that. I have anticipated his next several moves, and if things proceed as I expect, we may be sleeping in our beds by tomorrow night – the day after at the latest."

I have never known Holmes to be so wrong.

Chapter 21

After dinner, we returned to the hotel, once again using the tradesmen's entrance. As we sat in Holmes' room enjoying a cigar and a brandy, I said, "So what can we expect tomorrow?"

"I believe Roberts will attempt to arrange another meeting. We will, of course, agree, but we will set the place and the time." Holmes then lapsed into silence, and I could see that brain working, so I finished my brandy and decided to turn in.

As I reached the door, Holmes roused himself and said, "Whatever you do, do not answer the door. In fact, you may want to place a chair in front of the knob, just in case they have somehow managed to obtain a key."

"Better yet, why don't you rouse me early, and I will wait in here with you?"

"A capital idea, Watson."

Believing that the case would be over soon, I slept soundly and could hardly believe it when Holmes, in full Lord Chadwick makeup, shook me awake the next morning.

"My word, Watson. Your snores last night could have woken the dead."

"Sorry, old man. I hope I didn't keep you up."

"I remained awake all night, expecting that a message might be slipped under the door, but no such luck."

After I had washed and shaved, we were preparing to go downstairs for breakfast when there was a sudden rapping on the door.

"Who is it?" asked Holmes.

"I have a telegram for Lord Chadwick," said a rather young voice.

"Slip it under the door," Holmes replied.

"Yes, sir, but a reply by wire is requested."

After Holmes had read the telegram, he said, "Wait there, young man. I'll be with you in a minute."

Holmes then went to the desk and composed a short letter. He then opened the door so the lad could see him and gave the letter to the boy with a few coins. After the youngster had thanked Holmes and run off, I said, "Aren't you going to have him followed? Try to see who picks up the reply?"

"No. Consider, Watson, this needs to play itself out. You know that no one of import will pick up that telegram, and you also know that it will change hands at least half a dozen times in half a dozen different locales before it reaches someone of any significance.

"No, they will be on the alert – as would I if the situation were reversed. Better to let them think they have stolen a march and that Lord Chadwick is the only player with whom they must contend than to run the risk of exposing our plans too early."

"When you put it in that light …"

"There is no other way to play this; trust me, old friend."

"May I ask what your telegram said?"

"Certainly, I simply stated:

'*British Library Reading Room,*
Tomorrow 3; bring Cup;
No minions. '

"How can you be certain they will show up?"

"Because they desperately want what we have – the Alfred Jewel and the Lewis pawns."

"And will this mastermind be there?"

"That remains to be seen although I rather doubt such an esteemed personage would be concerned with mere commerce."

"So then we can arrest Roberts, but the big fish will escape."

"Perhaps, old friend, but trust me when I say that I have cast a rather wide net and if he should escape, the fault will be my own."

"So what's our next move?"

175

"We check out of here separately, and then I shall meet you back at Baker Street. Keep your wits about you," Holmes suggested. "We are nearing the end of this journey."

Then he added, "As I have a few things to which I must attend, I probably will not be home until dinner time."

Holmes then left, still disguised as Lord Chadwick, while I packed the few things I had brought to the hotel. At the front desk, I was told my bill had been settled. Although the doorman offered to arrange a cab for me, I followed Holmes' advice and chose the third cab in line.

As the cab turned onto Crestfield Street, I thought I saw a rather suspicious-looking figure loitering on the corner and keeping an eye on the front of the hotel. Although I couldn't identify him, I resolved to tell Holmes of my suspicions when I saw him at dinner that evening.

I spent the rest of the day catching up with those things I had neglected – including my practice – while masquerading as Lord Chadwick. Finally, shortly before six, I heard Holmes' tread on the stairs.

"So this will all be over in fewer than twenty-four hours?" I asked.

"One can but hope, Watson. If all goes according to my plans, it very well may be, but as the Scottish poet once observed, 'The best laid schemes o' mice an' men, gang aft agley.'"

"Well, that doesn't sound very optimistic."

"I am a realist, old friend. I sit here and try to put myself in my adversary's shoes. At the same time, that person is, no doubt, doing the same thing – putting himself in my shoes.

"I can see a way that this all ends as we would like it to, so I take steps to advance my cause. At the same time, he is taking steps to thwart my plans and plotting counter-moves of his own."

"You make it all seem so mechanical."

"And so it is – if you leave out the emotion. If there is an area where I have an advantage, that is it. You have described me, I believe as a 'thinking machine,' 'an automaton,' if you will."

"Yes, but I was only …"

"No need to apologize. In many senses, it is true. I take your words as a compliment to my abilities. Thus far the only person who might have bested me…"

"Moriarty!"

"Professor Moriarty is no more. I can only hope that his acolyte is not his equal. This is one instance where I hope the student has not surpassed the teacher; otherwise, this may turn into a protracted struggle, and I fear there may be unwanted casualties on both sides."

"I have faith in you, Holmes."

Ignoring the compliment, he rushed to the door to admit Mrs. Hudson, who had just arrived with our supper.

"No more talk of this tonight," he said. "I fear that we shall have our fill tomorrow."

We enjoyed a delicious dinner of braised salmon, potatoes and leeks and then relaxed with an after-dinner cigar and a glass of port.

After a prolonged silence, I said, "I suppose this will have to join the other cases in my tin dispatch box when it is over."

"I'm afraid so," replied Holmes. "Given the fact we know that forgeries are occupying places of pride in a number of museums around the world, including, of course, Britain, I have the feeling this may take years to sort out. Moreover, given Mycroft's involvement, as well as that of a number of other notables, I should think discretion would certainly trump everything else in this instance."

I had to laugh in spite of myself and agree that there was a large degree of truth in Holmes' sentiments.

We talked for some time about an array of topics, and finally Holmes said, "I have to rise early to take care of some business. I shall most certainly not see you at breakfast, but I will join you for lunch and then we shall proceed to the British Library."

"Just one question?"

"Only one?" replied Holmes with a smile.

"Who will be playing the role of Lord Chadwick?"

"At present, the role of Lord Chadwick is to be played by the esteemed John H. Watson, M.D. Of course, an understudy may assume the role if things do not go as I have planned. Not to worry, I shall attempt to take all contingencies into account."

Again, I slept soundly and Holmes was as good as his word, for I breakfasted alone. I was mulling over how this might play out and trying to see things as I imagined my friend visualized them, but to no avail.

Shortly after noon, I heard the front door open and a minute later Holmes entered the room, the picture of exuberance. "Things proceed apace," he informed me. "After we have dined, I will apply your makeup and brief you thoroughly on what I anticipate will happen in the Reading Room."

After a rather quick lunch, Holmes began filling me in on what he expected to transpire at the Library and how he wanted me to react. "They will not have the Nautilus Cup, so they will try to offer some other trinket in its place."

"You're certain of that?"

"Indeed! I wired Amsterdam again yesterday and received word this morning that the cup remains safe in a bank vault."

"Do you have any idea what they will offer in its stead?

"Not a clue, but you must demand the Mérode Cup as a pledge of their good faith."

"The Mérode Cup? But that's on display in the South Kensington Museum," I exclaimed.

"Is it?"

"You don't mean…"

"Of course I do. See how Roberts reacts when you insist upon it."

"Roberts? I thought I would be confronting the mastermind behind this whole plot."

"No, Watson. I had hoped that we might conclude this business today, but I have come to believe that this afternoon's theatrics are but the penultimate act. The finale, I hope, will be played out tomorrow in a place and at a time of our choosing."

"As for today, take a table in the center of the room. I expect there will be a fair number of people present. Select a book from a shelf, perhaps one of those sea adventures of which you seem so fond.

"Wait for Roberts to join you and let him begin the conversation.

"Ask to see the Nautilus Cup, and when he fails to produce it, get up to leave. I'm certain he will have an excuse as to why it is not there.

"Tell him he has one last chance to make things right. If anything is amiss at your next meeting, that will be the end of your dealings."

"Do you know where and when I should ask to meet?"

"Of course, and this is one of the most important lines you must deliver today." Holmes then told me to demand that the next meeting take place at noon the next day and when he told me the place I was dumbfounded.

"Are you certain that's where you want to conclude this business?"

"I am, and unless I miss my guess, Roberts will seize the opportunity. The second most important thing you must communicate to Roberts is that you will brook no intermediaries. Unless you meet with his superior, the transaction ends. Prior to that you might also want to hint that this could be the beginning of a long-term relationship – if the price is right and your conditions are met.

"Should he seem interested, and I am certain he will be, show him this." Holmes then placed a ring in my hand.

"Dare I ask where this came from?"

"It came from the court of the Ottonian emperors, who ruled central Europe from 936 until 1024. Dating from the late tenth or early eleventh century, this ring is a stunning example of Ottonian goldsmithing. At the center is a flowerlike ornament in cloisonné enamel. The ring bears witness to the high degree of sophistication of the goldsmiths of that region."

"No, I meant, how did you get it?"

"Oh, Mycroft was able to prevail upon a friend to loan it to him. Obviously it must be returned, so dangle it but do not exchange it or lose it."

"You can count on me."

"And where will you be while I am conducting this transaction?"

"Close by, old friend."

Finally, Holmes said, "The last key point that you must stress is this." He then told me word-for-word what he wished me to say.

All the while Holmes had been talking, he had been applying my disguise. After he had finished, he stepped back as was his wont and gave me a thorough inspection. "I don't need to remind you there's a great deal riding on your efforts this afternoon."

With that, he clapped me on the back, and said, "I almost forgot. You may need these." He then dashed into his room and returned with the two small wooden boxes that housed the Alfred Jewel and the Lewis pawns. I then headed downstairs where Holmes had arranged for a cab to pick me up at half two.

The ride to the British Library took about fifteen minutes. Opened in 1857, the room is a shrine to literacy. With its dome-like ceiling, which was inspired by the Pantheon in Rome, the room houses thousands of books. It is a stunning tribute to man's never-ending quest for knowledge and his constant attempts at self-improvement.

I wandered around the library for several minutes but I saw no one I recognized. I finally took the seat closest to the center at one of the spokes projecting out from the central desk.

After several minutes, I saw Roberts and another man enter the Reading Room. After looking around, he spotted me and a minute later, he had taken the seat next to mine. I noticed that the other man had seated himself directly across the way. Turning my attention to Roberts, I looked at him coldly and said, "Good day, sir," as I rose to leave.

"Your Lordship, I've just arrived. Where are you going?"

"You were given two instructions, sir, neither of which you appear to have followed. You were instructed to bring the Nautilus Cup and to arrive with your superior. Since you are here empty-handed, I can only assume that your mentioning the Cup was little more than a ploy of some sort. Also, since I am talking to you instead of your superior, I am left to conclude you disregarded that instruction as well. So I repeat, good day, sir."

"If Your Lordship will give me just two minutes. I will explain everything. The Nautilus Cup was purchased yesterday afternoon, and the buyer returned to the Continent last night. Surely, you can understand that he was loath to part with his purchase."

"And your superior?"

"Unavoidably detained."

"Pray tell, by what or by whom?"

"You are familiar with Sherlock Holmes?"

Suddenly, I felt my blood run cold. I was frightened for my friend, but I vowed to soldier on. "You mean that detective fellow?"

"The very same. We know he has got wind of our scheme, so as we speak my boss is leading him on a wild goose chase all over London …"

At that moment, Roberts paused as an elderly gentleman, a scholar by the looks of his bearing and the books he carried, passed by. Once he had left our aisle, Roberts continued his tale. "That detective may be smart, but my boss is smarter by far.

"Anticipating your reluctance, a meeting has been arranged for tomorrow night at St. Katherine Dock."

"I should much rather meet in the day at a more public place, and as I have purchased a train ticket for my journey back to Cambridge tomorrow evening, I am afraid that is out of the question."

I let that hang there for a few seconds, while Roberts weighed things over. Then I said, "If you can arrange a meeting to my liking, a bit earlier in the day, this could be the beginning of a long and prosperous partnership for both of us."

"What do you mean?"

Reaching into my waistcoat pocket, I extracted the ring Holmes had given me, "Surely, you can find a buyer for something like this?"

Roberts took the ring and examined it closely, "I can think of several parties who might be interested. Your price?"

Reaching over and retrieving the ring, I said, "We can determine that tomorrow."

Pointing to my case, I said, "I came here in good faith – with the Alfred Jewel and the Lewis pawns as promised. You have broken that faith, so tomorrow is your absolute last chance."

"When and where would Your Lordship like to meet?"

"Noon," and then I told him the location "We shall meet in the Chapter House in Westminster Abbey."

"Does Your Lordship really want to conduct business of this nature in such a public place?"

"Indeed, I do. It's open, and there is but one entrance, so I will know if you have the place filled with your men. If you do, I will just return to Cambridge."

"You are a most cautious man, Your Lordship."

"Which is why I have lived to tell the tale. And one further thing, since I may be leaving both the Alfred Jewel and the Lewis pawns with you, you must be prepared to compensate me with an item of equal or greater value."

"I am certain that can be arranged," he replied. "Did Your Lordship have a particular piece in mind?"

"Indeed I did, the Mérode Cup."

"The Mérode Cup," he exclaimed, "I am afraid that is impossible,"

"Nothing is impossible if you want it badly enough. How badly do you desire the Alfred Jewel and the pawns? If you treasure them as much as I think you do, you will bring the Mérode Cup, and please, do not insult my intelligence by bringing one of the copies you have made and are selling to private collectors all over Europe and in America."

"But Your Lordship, the Mérode Cup is currently on display in the South Kensington Museum."

Summoning up my best Holmes' impersonation, I smiled at him enigmatically and said only, "Is it?"

Chapter 22

I felt I had held my own in the exchange with Roberts, but more important I had dictated the terms of the next meeting. I watched as Roberts and his man left the library, and then I departed using a different entrance. I took great pains to make certain I wasn't followed.

I then took the cab to Victoria Station, where in the loo, I removed my makeup and emerged feeling much more like myself. I had entered from Belgrave Street and I exited onto Wilton Road where I hailed a cab that took me to Baker Street.

Holmes was waiting for me when I arrived. "From what I could see and hear, you did splendidly, old man. I must admit the ruffian that accompanied Roberts gave me a moment's pause, but you handled the situation with as much aplomb as could be expected."

I was dumbfounded by Holmes' remarks. While his praise, often doled out in miniscule doses, was greatly appreciated, I was disappointed in myself at not having ascertained his presence in the room. "You were there? I didn't see you."

"Surely, you remember an elderly scholar..."

"That was you?" I exclaimed. "I never suspected for a second."

"More important," laughed Holmes, "is that Roberts didn't either."

"So now we wait until tomorrow and capture Roberts and his boss at the Chapter House, and then we can put this whole sordid business behind us."

"I wish it were that simple, old friend. I am afraid we may have some work to do tonight, and I rather expect that we may be out quite late."

"Where are we going tonight?"

"I should think the answer would be obvious. In the meantime, I must attend to several pressing errands. I shall meet you back here for supper at seven, if that suits you?"

With that Holmes donned his hat and coat, grabbed a walking stick and descended the stairs. I strolled over to the window where I saw him hail a cab which clattered off in the direction of Bond Street. Although I toyed with the idea of writing, I decided – since it promised to be a late night and I wanted to be refreshed and ready – to take a short nap.

I was awakened by Holmes rapping on my door. "Watson, it is nearly seven, and dinner is served. I do hope that you will join me."

I threw some cool water on my face and joined Holmes at the table. "I must have been more tired than I thought," I said by way of explanation.

Holmes smiled and said, "No excuse is required, old friend. Rest is a great restorative. As a doctor, you should know that the body tells you what it requires."

"Indeed, I do, which makes me wonder why you keep disregarding the signals I know your body is sending you."

Holmes ignored my last remark and deftly changed the subject. "Everything is in place; now we can but hope that our foes see fit to cooperate."

"Cooperate? With you? Surely, you jest."

"Cooperate might not be the best word – perhaps oblige would be a more apropos choice."

"You want your foes to 'cooperate' and 'oblige' you?" I asked sarcastically.

"Well, they certainly won't be doing it knowingly," he countered. "Let's just say I hope no one throws a spanner in the works."

"Much better," I offered. "Come, Holmes, you would have taken me to task if I had put such words in your mouth in one of my literary endeavours."

"Perhaps," he smiled. "At any rate, if you should ever decide to set pen to paper about this particular case, I pray you, please omit the previous conversation in its entirety."

"I make no promises. After all, I am duty bound to provide my readers with the unvarnished truth."

This time I changed the subject. "Dark clothing, I assume, and bring my pistol as well?"

"Watson, you are positively scintillating of late. Another bravura performance in the reading room and now you read my thoughts as I have so often done yours."

By this time, we had finished dinner and as Holmes poured himself coffee and lit a cigarette, I wondered what the night might hold.

As I gazed at my friend, who sat there smoking, I realized that while he was attempting to appear nonchalant, his mind was working feverishly – examining and evaluating various scenarios and the outcomes that might result from each. I knew better than to disturb him during such periods of enormous concentration, so I contented myself with H. Rider Haggard's *Montezuma's Daughter*. Although I was enjoying the book, I thought it paled by comparison to his earlier *King Solomon's Mines*.

So engrossed had I become in the adventures of Thomas Wingfield in the New World that I was startled when Holmes interrupted my reverie by declaring, "It is time to go, Watson."

"And where exactly is it we are going? You still haven't told me."

"Why to foil a theft, of course," he replied.

"Of course, I should have known that." I confess that I believe that bit of sarcasm was lost on Holmes; either that, or it was ignored.

We descended the stairs and stepped outside to a rather warm evening. There was little moonlight, and the promise of showers was in the air. Waiting for us at the curb was a handsome Clarence with a driver and two black stallions. Holmes said nothing to the driver as we climbed into the coach. Obviously, this had all been pre-arranged.

We had been riding for about twenty minutes when I saw that we were passing Hyde Park. At that point I realized we were heading in the direction of both Madame Pittorino's shop and the South Kensington Museum. As I was uncertain, which of those, if either, would be our final destination, I remained silent.

When the carriage turned onto Watt's Way, I was certain that the antiques store was our destination, but we drove right past it and the cab stopped at the corner of Exhibition Road. We alighted from the Clarence, and Holmes turned to me and said, "From now on, silence is of the utmost importance."

We walked down the road a short while and then turned into the Royal College of Science building. As you might expect, it was deserted and we soon exited the rear and found ourselves behind the museum. Holmes walked to the back of the museum and pulled a key from his pocket. I looked at him curiously because I had been expecting him to pick the lock.

He saw my expression and smiled. "These are new locks, only recently installed, designed to deter the run-of-the-mill thief. I might have picked it, but Mycroft was kind enough to supply the key."

"What is this?" I asked.

"The tradesmen's entrance," he replied. "I am expecting company, but, truth be told, I have no idea when or from what direction they will arrive."

Once inside the museum, it was as though we had stepped into a deep abyss. The darkness was impenetrable, but Holmes lit a vesta and looked to his left. "Here they are, as promised." With that he bent down and retrieved two dark lanterns from the floor.

"Mycroft?" I whispered.

"At my instructions," replied Holmes.

After he lit the candles, he pulled the shutters half closed. As a result, we had enough light to navigate – but just barely.

I followed my friend as he made his way through the museum. The confident manner in which he walked told me he had rehearsed this excursion many times previously. At that point, I began to wonder how long Holmes had known that the final scene of this drama would play out here, but I remained silent.

Although I couldn't tell exactly where I was, I knew that we had made our way to the front of the museum. We passed through the various galleries in absolute silence, and when we passed the South Court, Holmes paused and turned to me.

"When we pass into the next gallery, we must find suitable hiding places. I have already arranged a bit of camouflage that I think will stand us in good stead, but you must remain vigilant. I have no idea when nor whence they will arrive, but there are plans in place. However, we are the point of the spear, as it were.

"It is now just past eleven. I do not expect anyone for at least two more hours, but I am hoping finally to take the offensive."

As we walked, Holmes' voice, speaking as softly as he was, still echoed through the cavernous rooms. Finally, we reached a long, narrow gallery. There were glass display cases on both sides of the room as well as a series of display cases running down the center of the room.

I now knew exactly where I was. Cupping my hands over his ear, I whispered, "This is the gallery where the Mérode Cup is displayed." Rather than answer, Holmes merely nodded. He then led me to a corner of the gallery and whispered, "This is where you will conceal yourself." Reaching down, he lifted a dark cloth from the corner. "Another gift from Mycroft," he explained. "Conceal yourself beneath the blanket and remain in the shadows.

"I shall be in a similar position at the other end of the gallery, in the corner diagonal from yours. When they enter, we will have them trapped between us."

"Holmes, how many people are you expecting?"

"I cannot say for certain. Two, perhaps three."

"And suppose we are outnumbered?"

"That is why I suggested you bring your pistol. The danger is that I may be accidentally struck by one of your bullets. So if you fire, do not aim for the lantern as I will be holding it directly in front of me."

"I understand, but I still think we are taking a terrible risk. Surely, there must be a better way."

"I wish there were, but we must catch them in the act; otherwise, our case is merely circumstantial, and I have little doubt that it would stand up under a jury's scrutiny – let alone a hostile barrister."

"I am certain you are correct, but you are taking a terrible chance."

"Watson, I have trusted you with my life in the past and have never had the slightest regret nor hesitation. Tonight is no different, old friend. Now, stay alert and no napping lest we be undone by an ill-timed snore."

I smiled in the darkness and said, "You can count on me."

I then nestled into the corner and covered myself with the cloth. It was lightweight, but totally opaque. I tried to see if the light of my dark lantern could penetrate it, but it was unable.

I heard Holmes walk towards his hiding place then stop by the display case. He did something in the dark, but I couldn't see what, and I was afraid of breaking the silence. A moment or two later, I heard him settle into place and then an eerie silence descended on the room.

Holmes and I had endured such vigils on several occasions. I remembered waiting on the moor for the hound that had menaced the Baskerville family to appear. I also recalled another sleepless night spent in a bank vault as we waited for John Clay to tunnel into the basement from below.

On those occasions, I had had company. Tonight I felt as though I were the last man on Earth. We could not speak nor communicate in any way and with that cloth shroud over me, I felt as though I had been entombed.

As you might expect, the time passed slowly; seconds seemed like minutes and minutes like hours. I was afraid to look at my watch, lest the light give my position away in the event that I had not heard the thieves enter.

Suddenly, after what seemed an eternity, I thought I heard a voice. I listened but as I heard nothing else, I decided I must have been mistaken. I was beginning to think I had imagined the sound, when from the next gallery, I heard someone whisper, "Almost there."

I readied myself but knew I had to wait for Holmes' signal. Suddenly the voice was no more than five feet away, when it exclaimed *sotto voce,* "Here we are – at last!"

Chapter 23

Since I hadn't heard any footsteps, I guessed that they must be wearing rubber-soled shoes. The voices were now some fifteen to twenty feet away, I judged, so I peeked around the side of my blanket. Unfortunately, my view was blocked by the display case, but I could definitely discern at least two pairs of legs in the soft glow given off by the dark lamps they carried.

"Here it is! Beautiful, isn't it?" one of the robbers exclaimed. I thought I recognized the voice as belonging to our old friend, Roberts, but I couldn't be absolutely sure.

Then the other voice said, "Get on with it." I didn't recognize the voice immediately, but I thought there was something familiar about it. It was muffled and then I realized the speaker must be wearing a mask.

All of a sudden, the first voice, the one I believed to be Roberts, said, "That's queer."

"What is?"

"The key won't fit in the lock."

"Are you sure?"

"It's a bloody lock. It doesn't require a great deal of skill to open it. Would you care to try?"

"No. Perhaps they changed all the locks recently. Just take your gun and smash the glass. The sooner we are out of here, the better I will feel."

I then heard a bang, followed by another, and then a third. "I don't understand; the glass won't break."

"Are you hitting it hard enough?"

"I'm afraid if I swing too hard, I'll not only shatter the glass but damage the Cup. Do you want me to try and shoot through it from an angle?"

"No. If the bullet should ricochet and damage the Cup, we have nothing to give to Lord Chadwick. Keep hitting it with your gun. It must break sooner or later."

Suddenly, I heard a familiar voice say, "The glass will most certainly break eventually, but not before you are enjoying the company of your fellow prisoners at Newgate."

"Sherlock Holmes!" I heard the voice I thought belonged to Roberts exclaim. "But how? What are you doing here?"

"Why, I am here to prevent you from stealing the Mérode Cup. I should have thought that rather obvious."

"And just how is it you intend to stop me? From what I can see, you are armed with nothing but a cane while I am holding a pistol. It is hardly a fair match, I think you'd agree."

"Most certainly, but Dr. Watson has brought his pistol as well, and he has it trained on you right now."

As Holmes was speaking, I had extricated myself from the blanket and stood upright. I also edged my way across the gallery thus eliminating the prospect of Holmes getting caught in the crossfire. From my new position, I could now see that my instincts had been correct, and Roberts was indeed the speaker. His companion, who had remained silent during the exchange with Holmes, was wearing a mask and thus impossible to identify. The only thing I could tell for certain was that he was not nearly as tall as Roberts.

Roberts took a quick look over his shoulder and saw me standing there with my gun aimed squarely at him. Half turning to me, he continued to speak to Holmes, "It appears we have a standoff of some sort. Dr. Watson shoots me and I shoot you, or perhaps I shoot you first and then Dr. Watson shoots me. In either event, it appears that your side may well emerge victorious, but it will be a Pyrrhic victory, of that I can assure you."

"It need not end that way," countered Holmes, "you can lay down your weapon and live."

"You call spending the rest of my life in prison living," snarled Roberts. "I can assure you, Mr. Holmes, that is not living but a living death. And with my luck, I'll end up on the gallows. No, sir, I think I'll take my chances tonight and give the dice one more roll."

What happened next was a blur. It all transpired in just a second or two – everything seemed to be occurring simultaneously. As a result, the telling of it will take far longer than the actual events.

Having said his piece, I watched as Roberts nudged his companion as though he wanted to speak to him. After a few whispered words, which I could not hear, he suddenly whirled and flung his lantern directly at Holmes just as his companion threw his own light at me. Holmes made an effort to deflect the lamp with his own lantern and was partially successful, but as they smashed together, both lights went out.

The lamp hurled at me was thrown oddly and without a great deal of force, so I managed to get off a shot before it struck me in the shoulder. Immediately after that I heard glass shatter and then a second shot rang out.

"Holmes! Holmes! Are you all right?"

Before he answered, I thought I felt someone rush by me in the darkness, but in all the confusion, I couldn't be certain.

"I'm all right, Watson, but we need light," Holmes exclaimed. I was so relieved to hear his voice that I followed his orders without thinking. I retrieved my dark lantern from the corner where I had left it and struck a vespa. After lighting the candle and opening the shutter, I saw Holmes kneeling over the figure of Roberts. There was a growing pool of blood on the floor, and I knew that at least my shot had been true.

"Is he?"

"Yes, old friend. He's dead."

"I have never taken a life before ..."

"And you still haven't," Holmes said.

"But I fired."

"Yes, and so did his partner."

"But my bullet..."

"Broke that display case over there," said Holmes, indicating a tall case in the corner that housed several daggers and various other artifacts.

"How can you be certain?"

"Look at his shirt," he said, as he shone his lantern directly on the man's shirt. "He was shot once in the heart at extremely close range, so close, in fact, that you can see the powder burns on the cloth," said Holmes, indicating a singed circle on the dead man's chest.

"My word, then his partner shot him. But why?"

"Presumably to prevent him from talking. Remember, Watson, I told you there was someone pulling the strings, directing Roberts' every move."

"Well, in all the confusion, I thought I felt someone rush by in the darkness."

"That was, no doubt, the mastermind behind Roberts."

"Well, he's escaped then. And since we don't know his identity how will we ever catch him?"

"Not to worry, old friend. Just before I took my position, I sprinkled the floor with a very fine mixture of talcum power. Be careful, you don't want to step in that footprint."

Looking down, I saw the clear outline of at least two rubber-soled shoes, of differing sizes, in the powder that Holmes had spread liberally all over that section of the floor. I also noticed several footprints that were headed in the direction where I had been hidden. "So I was right," I thought. "He did run by me."

Turning to Holmes, I said, "But you can't convict someone based on a footprint."

"No, but I can eliminate several suspects by examining shoe sizes. Now, while I conduct my investigation here, why don't you go fetch Lestrade."

"You want me to go to Scotland Yard?"

"That won't be necessary. You see, an hour after we took up our positions, I arranged for Lestrade and several of his best men to surround the building surreptitiously.

"I shouldn't be surprised if the Inspector isn't holding court right now, telling anyone who'll listen how he devised this brilliant plan to outwit the criminal genius who succeeded Moriarty.

"Although I have my suspicions as to whom he has captured, I think we should advise the Inspector about this body and the events that have transpired."

As I left in search of Lestrade, I looked back and saw Holmes striding across the gallery. I had no idea what he was doing, but the last thing I saw him do was run from the case with the cup to the place where I had concealed myself.

By the light of the dark lantern, I made my way to the front entrance of the museum, and when I pushed open the heavy oak door, I heard a cacophony of police whistles and then a familiar voice ordered, "Don't you move! You are under arrest."

"Stand down, Lestrade. It's Dr. Watson," I said.

Upon hearing that, the Inspector emerged from the shadows along with a rather capable-looking constable. "Good evening, Doctor. I thought I heard two gun shots earlier."

"You did indeed, Inspector. One man has been killed. Holmes is with the body. He sent me to fetch you."

At that point, Holmes emerged from the front door. "You shot one of the thieves, Mr. Holmes?"

"Not I, Inspector. A man we had come to know as John Roberts was shot and killed by his accomplice. Has anyone else emerged from the museum?"

"Not by this door, I can vouch for that." Turning to the constable, he said, "Shaw, go check with the other men and be quick about it." After the burly constable had left, Lestrade said, "I did just as you instructed, Mr. Holmes and stationed men outside every door."

After about ten minutes, Shaw returned, "Well?" demanded Lestrade.

"No one saw anyone come out, and Constable Jenkins appears to be missing."

"What do you mean, 'missing'? Wasn't he assigned to the exit by the South Court?"

"Yes, sir, but he's not there now."

"We are dealing with a most dangerous foe, Lestrade, who has already killed once tonight. I'm sure a second murder would be of little consequence if it meant his freedom."

We then made our way to the right side of the building, and after a few minutes, Holmes exclaimed, "Over here, Lestrade."

We all ran to the glow of his lantern and there in the shadows lie the body of a young police constable. Shaw began to blow his police whistle furiously. Even without a close examination, I could see that like Roberts, Jenkins had been shot once at close range. As Holmes and Lestrade bent over the body, I saw the powder burns on his tunic and knew the killer had claimed another life.

"This is intolerable," exclaimed Lestrade.

"Trust me, Inspector, I want this murderer brought to justice every bit as badly as you do. But our killer is clever, resourceful and merciless. Fortunately, time is an enemy to this fiend, not a friend."

"What do you mean, Mr. Holmes?"

"I mean to bring this killer to justice in the very near future. Right now, our foe feels safe. The law has been outwitted, and he has escaped, but I promise you, Lestrade, his freedom will be short-lived."

"I only hope you are right, Mr. Holmes."

"I will not rest until justice has been served. You may count on that."

By now the other constables had gathered, so Holmes and I left them to their shared grief. As we walked towards Baker Street, looking vainly for a cab, I said to Holmes, "That is certainly not what I expected this evening."

"Nor I, Watson. I thought I had accounted for all contingencies, but I failed to consider the utter ruthlessness of our quarry. Rest assured, old friend, that is a mistake, I will never make again."

From the tone of his voice and the set of his jaw, I knew that justice would be visited upon this killer, and I decided that if I were able to avoid doing one thing in life, it would be running afoul of Sherlock Holmes.

Chapter 24

I slept until nearly midday and when I awoke, there was no sign of Holmes. As Mrs. Hudson served my lunch, she remarked, "You and Mr. Holmes had quite the late night. It was nearly four when you arrived home."

"I'm sorry to have awakened you."

"No need to apologize, Doctor. I had a devil of a time falling asleep myself. But I thought if you two were out until such an hour that you'd be wanting sleep more than breakfast. And in your case, I was right."

"And in the case of Mr. Holmes?"

"He came down around eight, and asked just for coffee. I brought him up a tray and then I heard him go out about an hour later."

I knew better than to ask if Holmes had given any indication of his destination, so I ate a solitary lunch and then began to read the papers. After that I set out for my office. My colleague, Dr. Martins, had been so gracious in covering my practice that I felt I needed to explain my prolonged absence and apologize.

I also brought a bottle of cabernet sauvignon as a thank you, though in my mind, it was more a bribe than anything else. Fortunately, he was supplementing his income quite nicely – at my expense – and was quite cordial and somewhat relieved, I think, that my absence would continue for a few more days.

I returned home around four, and no sooner had I entered the sitting room then Holmes exclaimed, "There you are. I've been waiting for you."

Holmes seemed impervious to the fact that waiting could be construed as a two-way street and seeing that he was flushed with excitement, I held my piece. "What is going on?"

"We have a meeting tonight at seven. Our presence is requested, but I believe it may prove to be essential."

"With whom are we meeting? And what are we meeting about?"

Ignoring my questions, Holmes continued as though he hadn't heard me. "It is certainly not a formal occasion, but the matters to be considered are of grave import, so do dress accordingly."

With that, he turned to enter his bedroom. "Holmes, I think you could have the courtesy to answer my questions."

He looked totally befuddled, and I realized that in his own excitement, he had not heard me speak. After an awkward pause, he said, "What questions?"

"With whom are we meeting? And what are we meeting about?"

"We are to meet with the members of the acquisitions committee of the South Kensington Museum. There is a conference room next to the director's office where small gatherings, such as this one, are held quite regularly." In saying that, he seemed to think he had supplied the answers to all the questions I might have – even though I had at least twenty more – and so he turned and strode into his bedroom, closing the door behind him.

I stood there mystified, knowing that I had missed something significant, perhaps several somethings, all of which I assumed had been observed, evaluated and categorized by my friend.

With little else to do for more than an hour, I sat in my chair and approached the case in much the same way I thought Holmes might have. I considered everything, beginning with the note from Ralph Prescott, through the murder of Chester Boles, to our various meetings with the different personalities who had involved themselves, in one way or another, with this case.

My head was beginning to throb, when all of a sudden, Holmes emerged from his room and declared, "I do hope that is the aroma of chicken I detect wafting up from Mrs. Hudson's kitchen, for I am ravenously hungry."

Over a dinner of roast chicken, potatoes and green beans, Holmes was his usual charming self. He regaled me with stories about a few of his early cases, before we had joined forces. We had just finished our coffee, when he looked at his watch and said, "It's time to go."

We found a hansom waiting for us, and Holmes never spoke to the driver. Obviously, he too was playing a small role as my friend's plan came together. The streets were surprisingly empty, given the fair weather, and we made excellent time, arriving at the South Kensington Museum some fifteen minutes later. As it was a Friday, the museum was open later than usual.

As we walked through the galleries towards the director's office, I thought I spotted several familiar faces – Constable Shaw, who was not in uniform, among them – admiring the various artifacts and other pieces that were on display.

Finally, we reached the director's office and were shown into the small conference room adjacent to it

Lord Hargreaves was already seated at the head of the table, and Lord Howe occupied the chair immediately to his right. Upon seeing us, Lord Hargreaves rose and said, "Mr. Holmes, Dr. Watson, it is so good to see you again. I can only wish that it were under more felicitous circumstances."

Lord Howe had a very different reaction upon seeing us. "This is supposed to be a committee meeting for members only. Why are they here?"

Hargreaves looked at him and said forcefully, "They are here because I invited them."

The answer may not have satisfied Howe, but it did serve to silence him.

"We can begin as soon as Lord Danvers and Lady Cox arrive. I understand you are serving as a proxy of sorts for your brother, Mr. Holmes."

"That is true, Your Lordship. Mycroft has been unavoidably detained at Whitehall, and he has given me the power to vote in his stead, assuming, of course, that meets with the approval of the rest of the board."

Holmes, who had ignored Lord Howe's outburst, busied himself examining the various daguerreotypes, photographs, maps and illustrations that adorned the walls. At one point, he turned to Lord Hargreaves and remarked, "This is a most interesting map."

"Indeed," he replied, "it shows the various lands – northern Germany, Denmark and The Netherlands – which the Anglo-Saxons called home before they invaded our homeland in the fourth and fifth centuries. I'm sure I don't have to tell you Mr. Holmes that the initial incursions were beaten back by the Romans. How different things might have been had the legions remained here."

At that moment, both Lord Danvers and Lady Cox arrived together. Although she was talking to Danvers as they entered, and her back was to us, I could hear her words quite clearly, "I simply cannot believe how rude people are. What is this world coming to?"

Since Danvers was facing in our direction, he spoke first, saying, "Sorry, we are a bit late, but the traffic was quite alarming, and then Lady Cox had a rather untoward encounter with one of the visitors."

"Odd," I thought to myself, "the streets were empty when we drove here. I wonder what might have happened."

At that point Lady Cox retorted, "Untoward? I think rude would describe it far better. The first fellow almost knocked me over, and his companion was an even bigger oaf." Suddenly realizing that we were present, her face brightened considerably, and she said, "I see we have visitors. Might we expect a special presentation of some sort?"

"Not exactly," said Hargreaves. "If everyone will please be seated we can call this meeting to order."

Danvers sat to Hargreaves' left, and Lady Cox took the seat next to him. Holmes sat next to her while I sat across from my friend leaving an empty chair between Lord Howe and myself.

"If no one has any objections," began Hargreaves, "Mr. Sherlock Holmes will serve as proxy for his brother. Concerns, anyone?"

"I still don't think it's right," Howe said. "They aren't members," he continued indicating Holmes and myself.

"So we have one 'nay.' Lord Danvers? Lady Cox?" Hargreaves asked.

"I have no issue with one Holmes taking the place of another," said Lady Cox.

"Nor do I," agreed Danvers.

"So the motion is carried," Hargreaves continued. "Mr. Holmes, Dr. Watson, you are welcome here."

"I voted for Holmes," said Danvers testily. "I never thought Dr. Watson would be remaining as well." He then objected to my continued presence but was again voted down by a margin of three to one.

"Now that the matter of their presence," said Hargreaves, gesturing to Holmes and myself, "has been settled, let us turn to more pressing matters. As I am sure you have heard by now, there was an attempt made early this morning to steal the Mérode Cup. Fortunately, Mr. Holmes and Dr. Watson were able to thwart the thieves. Sadly, two men, one of the burglars and a Scotland Yard constable, were killed during the robbery attempt."

"That's dreadful," exclaimed Lady Cox. "These men must be caught and punished."

"Trust me," I replied, "Mr. Holmes and Scotland Yard are leaving no stone unturned in their quest for justice."

"Obviously, we are grateful that you were there, but how is it that both of you came to be in the museum this morning?" asked Howe.

"I was there, along with Dr. Watson, because I expected there would be an attempt made to steal the Mérode Cup. Fortunately, the new locks and specially tempered glass, ordered by my brother, Mycroft, slowed the thieves down. Unfortunately, in the darkness and confusion, one was killed and the other escaped."

At that moment, there was a knock on the door. Hargreaves rose, answered it and said, "There is a gentleman here who insists upon speaking with you Mr. Holmes. He says it will take but a minute."

While Holmes excused himself, Howe continued his questioning. "Can you tell us, Dr. Watson, how Mr. Holmes knew exactly when the thieves would strike?"

"We didn't know exactly," I confessed. "As a matter of fact, we had quite a long, uncomfortable wait until they finally arrived."

"Yes," he persisted, "but how did you know to expect them last night?"

"I had set a trap, and they took the bait," replied Holmes as he walked through the door to rejoin us. You see, Lord Howe, it has been my experience that most thieves, while they might be deemed clever, lack real imagination."

"What do you mean?" interrupted Howe.

"Quite simply this. A clever thief can steal something and get away with it. Planning is required and perhaps a bit of courage, but such a theft requires little more than that. Now, a thief with imagination will steal something and do it in such a manner that no one even suspects the item in question has been taken."

"How is that possible?" inquired Hargreaves, who seemed genuinely interested.

"One way is by taking the priceless original and leaving a worthless copy in its place."

"That seems to me an inordinately difficult task."

"With careful planning and a little assistance from the powers that be, such a theft is far easier than you might imagine."

"You talk as if such thefts are commonplace," said Lady Cox. "As if they were occurring on a regular basis."

To say that Holmes' next words induced pandemonium in such a small area would not even begin to do his utterance justice. Still, that is exactly what happened when he strode to the opposite end of the table from Lord Hargreaves and proclaimed,

"Such thefts have been occurring at this museum for a period of several months, perhaps as long as a year. The thief has had a compatriot inside the museum, telling him what to steal and when, and in some cases even lending a hand by providing him with access and keys to the display cases. I believe it entirely possible, nay probable, that on more than one occasion, this person has actually removed select items and replaced them with cleverly forged imitations."

Holmes then paused in his declaration, I am sure more for dramatic effect than anything else, and proclaimed, "However, I assure you this ends tonight as the thief is among us."

Chapter 25

With Holmes' final pronouncement, the room erupted in an unmitigated babel. If I recall correctly, Lord Howe was threatening to sue Holmes for slander while Lord Danvers was yelling, at the top of his lungs, for proof and threatening to give Holmes a "good hiding."

Lacking a gavel, Lord Hargreaves resorted to banging the table with the palm of his hand and bellowing for order in an effort to be heard above the din. Of the board members, only Lady Cox retained her sense of decorum, refusing to join in the fray that appeared dangerously close to devolving into an all-out donnybrook.

By contrast, to the other men, Holmes appeared to be enjoying the disharmony he had sown, and I could swear so placid was his expression that I knew he was making every effort to refrain from smiling. For myself, I sat there taking it all in and wondering how it was going to end up.

After several minutes, the clamor had abated and Lord Hargreaves was finally able to restore some semblance of order. Staring at Holmes, he said icily, "Mr. Holmes, you have leveled a number of serious allegations. I do hope that you have ample proof to convince us of their veracity. I also hope you will be kind enough to identify any and all guilty parties so they may be prosecuted."

"I propose to do both," replied Holmes, "but please, as I so often encourage those who seek out my services to do, I intend to begin at the beginning. Holmes then commenced the tale with the death of Ralph Prescott, followed in short order by the murder of Chester Boles.

"At that point, I could see the game; Museums and private collectors all over Europe were being sold counterfeits of legendary *objets d'art.* Although I thought I knew how the substitutions were being handled, I lacked proof."

"And just how were these so-called 'substitutions' of yours accomplished?" sneered Lord Howe.

"It was a matter of some simplicity," replied Holmes, "and yet it required a certain daring that raised simplicity to brilliance. You see, everything hinged upon a group of talented supporting players. These included a brilliant young engineer, with an incredible gift for physics, who saw her academic work funded so long as she was willing to supply certain pieces. So just as she labored to create new and improved lenses for telescopes, she also created *plique à jour* panels, platters, gold cups with lids and various other pieces.

"Those in turn were passed to a talented jeweler, with a fondness for the turf. A craftsman extraordinaire, he created at least eight Mérode Cups, of which I am aware – although there may well be more – that now reside in the galleries of some of the most esteemed private collectors around the world. All these collectors believe they possess the original while the one residing here in the museum is a forgery.

"He also created assorted bracteates which now grace various collections, and in some cases museums."

"Whenever they wished for more, they simply borrowed the original from the museum and used it as a model for their castings."

"But why not leave a copy here and just keep the original?" asked Lord Hargreaves.

"That may have been part of the plan, but as museums are constantly loaning items to other museums, they couldn't take the chance that the copy would be detected. Such a discovery could lead to a widespread investigation, and there's no telling how many counterfeits might be discovered."

"But the dead men, you mentioned, how do they fit into it?" asked Lady Cox.

"There I must venture into the realm of conjecture – something I am always loath to do as Dr. Watson will attest. I believe that the jeweler, Chester Boles, was killed because he became a liability. Perhaps he wanted a larger share for his efforts. It's difficult to say why without facts, but a jeweler could be easily replaced if the price were right."

"And the other fellow? The one who died in your rooms?"

"His name was Ralph Prescott. He was also working with members of a group who were endeavouring to bring the ring to justice. I believe, and here again we venture into conjecture, that Prescott had successfully infiltrated the ring. At his post mortem, we discovered he was smuggling certain drawings in his artificial leg. Drawings that appeared to be copies of items that were being counterfeited. In a second secret compartment in that same leg, we also found a rather large diamond dating from the late medieval period, cut in a fashion typical of that era.

"However, the most telling object in Prescott's possession was a small sack which contained a number of pieces of imitation *plique à jour*. Once set in a piece they could not be removed without possibly doing irreparable damage to the piece and thus rendering it worthless. As a result, there was no definitive method to ascertain whether anyone's copy of the

Mérode Cup were genuine without risking such damage, something any true antiquarian would be unwilling to do. As I said, it was simplicity bordering on brilliance.

"When I began to examine this case, I knew that somehow those glass-like pieces would come into play. And that set me to thinking and wondering how I might turn that to my advantage. More important, however, is that the bogus *plique à jour* pieces provided me with the impetus to follow a specific path, and that journey has ended here tonight with this meeting."

"That's all well and good," said Lord Howe, "but as you have said twice, all you have is conjecture. I would respectfully suggest that if you have something concrete to offer then get to it; otherwise, let's call in the police and let them sort it out. After all," he added derisively, "they are professionals."

"My conjecture dealt only with the reasons why Boles and Prescott were murdered. As far as the killer is concerned, I believe we have more than enough proof to possibly send that individual to the gallows and, barring that, to a life sentence.

"As to the murderer, it had to be someone connected to the museum. Someone with ready access to the various exhibits – and more important, someone who possessed a set of keys."

"Well, none of us has keys except Hargreaves," shouted Lord Howe. And with that everyone in the room, but Holmes, began to glare at the director.

"Rest assured, Lord Hargreaves has been a loyal and faithful servant to this institution," said Holmes.

"Last night, as I told you, I was expecting an attempt on the Mérode Cup, so before the thieves arrived I sprinkled some raw cacao powder on the floor. I was hoping to ascertain the shoe sizes of the thieves as an additional piece of evidence. However, my plan worked better than expected because it was readily apparent that the thief who escaped had very small feet. In fact, the footprints were so small they confirmed what I had long suspected – the mastermind behind this entire enterprise was a woman. Isn't that so, Lady Cox?"

This time, all eyes turned towards Lady Cox. Calmly, she looked at my friend and said without any emotion, "Mr. Holmes, you will be hearing from my solicitor, I assure you."

"It won't do, Lady Cox. You must give this up now."

"You have footprints that you believe to be a woman's and on that basis you accuse me of theft and murder. I fear you are the one who must give it up, Mr. Holmes."

"Did I neglect to mention the books?"

Now it was my turn to be amazed, but before I could blurt out the question on everyone's mind, Lord Danvers asked, "To what books are you referring, Mr. Holmes?"

"Among the many volumes in Lady Cox's rather exhaustive library, there are two that caught my attention. To the best of my knowledge she is the only person who possesses both *A Treatise on the Binomial Theorem* as well as *The Dynamics of an Asteroid.*

"Should you not be familiar with those works, they were both penned by the late Professor James Moriarty."

"But anyone with an interest in mathematics might have those books," protested Lord Howe.

"True," said Holmes, "but how many people would have copies signed by the Professor and inscribed 'To my most brilliant pupil'?"

Chapter 26

Holmes continued, "Lady Cox, since I have learned you never attended university, I can only conclude that you were a brilliant student in some other field. Crime, perhaps?"

"James warned me about you, Mr. Holmes" Lady Cox said as she reached into her bag and withdrew a small revolver. "However, he assured me he would take care of you when the time was right.

"I must say, he was right: You are clever. I certainly didn't expect you to be waiting for us last night."

I must admit I don't know which surprised me more: Lady Cox brandishing a revolver or her referring to the late Professor Moriarty as James.

Suddenly Holmes interrupted my thoughts, "A question, if I may."

"Since every condemned man is entitled to a last wish, I will assume this is yours. You may ask me anything, and if the answer is not too embarrassing, I will answer it."

"Why did you accompany Roberts? You could have sent two men and remained in the clear."

"I must confess, Roberts, who was capable in so many areas, ultimately became something of a disappointment. For all his talent as a thief, the man had scruples. He refused to kill anyone. I had to dispatch one of my more capable lieutenants to deal with Boles, while I dosed Prescott with strychnine myself perhaps an hour or two before his requested meeting with you.

"Had you met him on time, well, Lord knows what he might have told you.

"Roberts also had the opportunity to kill both you and Dr. Watson, and thus avoid this entire spectacle – yet here you are. As a result, I could no longer trust him. Had I dispatched him to the museum with another man, I am certain he would have brought me the Mérode Cup, but I am equally certain that some other trinket would have found its way into his pocket, with him thinking me none the wiser."

"But why shoot him?"

"I should think that's obvious. I have no doubt that if he were captured, he would have told you everything if it meant his life. He left me no choice."

The utter lack of emotion in that last statement cut me to the quick. It was obvious that she had murdered before and would do so again – with little or no compunction. I looked at her eyes and saw only ice. I realized human life meant nothing to her.

"Now, gentlemen, if you cooperate, I will attempt to make this as painless as possible."

"And if we do not?" I said.

"Then you will suffer, a slow, agonizing death, and I will enjoy watching every minute of it. I think Dr. Watson will agree that few deaths are as painful as being shot in the stomach and bleeding to death."

"If we rush her, she can't shoot us all," said Lord Hargreaves. However, as she had been speaking, Lady Cox had risen from her seat and backed all the way across the room.

"You may certainly attempt that, Your Lordship, but I must warn you that I am an excellent shot, and I will drop all of you before you have taken two steps. And as most of you know, I am a woman of my word."

"I'm inclined to believe her," said Lord Howe. "I've been shooting with her, and she is an excellent marksman."

Lady Cox nodded, "Thank you, James. I am so glad you remember."

"Yes, well that's all fine and good," said Holmes, "but I fear you have overlooked one thing?"

"Oh, and what would that be Mr. Holmes?"

"Bullets." With that Holmes began to reach into his pocket.

"Not so fast, Mr. Holmes."

"Madam, I assure you I am unarmed. I am merely reaching into my pocket because there is something I wish you to see." With that he then held out his hand towards Lady Cox. From where I was sitting, I could see that in his palm he held a number of bullets. "I believe these belong to you."

For the first time, I saw a look of uncertainty pass across Lady Cox's face. "You're bluffing, Mr. Holmes. It hardly suits you."

"Madam, I never bluff," said my friend who then strode across the room. As he did so, Lady Cox kept firing the revolver aiming for my friend, but the only noise it made was a harmless "Click, click, click."

Suddenly, Holmes reached out and seizing her wrist, twisted it, forcing her to drop the gun. She screamed and tried to claw his face, but the pressure on her wrist was unrelenting. Turning to me, Holmes said, "Watson, if you would summon Inspector Lestrade."

"I assume he is outside in the waiting room."

Holmes smiled and nodded, "You assume correctly, old friend."

So I opened the door, and there I found Lestrade and two plainclothesmen sitting in absolute silence. "Is it over?" Lestrade asked when he saw me.

"I believe it is," I replied.

As they entered the room, I heard Lady Cox screech, "You! You! It can't be."

Then Lestrade said, "Lady Ashley Cox, in the name of the Queen, I am arresting you for the murder of one James Roberts and the attempted murder of Mr. Sherlock Holmes. Other charges may be filed at a later date. Finally, I should warn you that anything you say may be used against you."

He then placed a pair of darbies on her wrists and led her from the room. As she reached the door, she turned and hissed at my friend, "This isn't over yet, Mr. Holmes – not by a long shot."

"Mr. Holmes, I don't know how to thank you," said Lord Hargreaves. "The museum and I – and I'm certain the others feel the same – owe you a debt that can never be repaid." He then followed Lestrade and Lady Cox out of the room.

"Think nothing of it," said Holmes.

"But how did you get the bullets from her gun?" stammered Lord Danvers.

"Actually, I didn't," replied Holmes. "In that area, I had some help, courtesy of an old friend."

"I'm not certain I follow," I offered.

"I fully expected Lady Cox to be armed. After all, a woman in her position has made enemies on both sides of the law."

"Uneasy lies the head that wears the crown," I said.

Holmes gave me a look then a smile and said, "Exactly. You will recall that when Lady Cox arrived she complained about being jostled by two men. And when Lestrade and his officers entered to arrest her, she screamed 'You!'

"She recognized the officer who had nearly knocked her over. What she failed to realize is that was merely a diversion. While she was getting knocked about, Willie Blaine, perhaps the most talented pickpocket it has ever been my misfortune to encounter, removed her revolver from her bag, emptied the bullets and replaced it – all without her being any the wiser.

"When I was summoned to the door, that was Willie who handed me the bullets and assured me that the gun was indeed empty. So you see, I faced no danger; however, had Willie not been successful, things might have taken a decidedly different turn."

"Did you have a contingency plan, Mr. Holmes?" asked Lord Danvers.

Answering for my friend, I said, "Of course he did. He probably had several – after all, this is Sherlock Holmes we are talking about."

Although Holmes waved me off dismissively, I could tell that he was touched by the compliment. "I did have another avenue to explore had Willie failed," Holmes admitted.

At that point, Lord Hargreaves reentered the room carrying a bottle. "Normally, we have only tea or coffee at these meetings. I have been saving this for a special occasion," he said holding up a bottle of Glenturret, "and this certainly qualifies a special occasion."

As I admired the bottle, Lord Hargreaves informed me, "This comes from the oldest distillery in Scotland." His tone softened as he added, "Although I must admit that claim is disputed by at least two other distillers."

Going to the sideboard, he poured each of us a dram, handed out the glasses and then said, "I should like to propose a toast to Mr. Sherlock Holmes.'"

After a chorus of "Here, here," we drank to Holmes' health. I could see that he was feeling uncomfortable, and when Lord Hargreaves went to refill our glasses, Holmes declined, much to my chagrin, as the whisky was truly excellent.

"Dr. Watson and I must be up early tomorrow," replied Holmes. "Duty calls."

When we had departed and were safely ensconced in a cab on our way back to Baker Street, I said to Holmes, "Duty calls? Do we have another case of which I am not aware?"

"Not yet, Watson, but as you so ably attested, "I like to plan for all possibilities."

I had to laugh despite myself and before Holmes lapsed into silence, I informed him, "Holmes, I have said it before and I'll say it again, you are truly incorrigible."

Chapter 27

Once we had settled into our chairs in the sitting room, whisky and cigars in hand, I turned to Holmes and asked, "When did you first begin to suspect Lady Cox?"

"I suspected her as soon as I saw Moriarty's books on her shelves. After all, who, besides a devotee, would treasure a bound copy of a thesis on the binomial theorem – especially one written by a then-unknown and unheralded twenty-one year old mathematician? And when I saw the inscriptions, I was certain. Unfortunately, as you are well aware, there is a huge gap between knowing and proving."

"Indeed, there were so many threads to untangle, but you did a masterful job."

"Well, there are still a few loose ends to tie up."

"Are there?"

"We must return the Alfred Jewel to Mycroft and the Lewis chessmen to Madame Pittorino. And then we must make inquiries about the diamond?"

"Diamond?"

"The one Prescott was carrying in his prosthesis."

"Holmes, you once asked, 'Why would a man carry an artificial form of glass that harkens to the medieval period as well as a real diamond from the same era? Further, why conceal one but not the other? And why would he hide the diamond and two drawings in an artificial limb?'"

"So I did. I think the answer can be found in the fact that the *plique à jour* pieces could always be replaced, but the diamond could not. So he kept it in the safest place he knew. One might search for a hidden compartment in the leg, without ever suspecting there were two."

"But you did."

"It is my nature to suspect everyone and everything," he replied.

"Is there anything else that need be addressed?"

"No, I believe that should tie up all the loose ends in this case. I will see if I can persuade Mycroft to reimburse the churches for the items that were stolen. After all, I should think 'the government' can well afford such a small sum, given what was at stake."

The next morning, Holmes received a wire at breakfast. Upon ripping it open and reading it, he looked at me and said, "If you are not busy, Mycroft would like us to meet him at the Diogenes Club at half seven."

"I wouldn't miss it," I replied. After a busy day at my practice, I met Holmes at Baker Street where, after dinner, we decided to stroll to the Diogenes Club. Upon arriving, we were ushered into the Stranger's Room, where we were joined a few minutes later by Mycroft Holmes.

After settling his bulk into a wing chair, he asked if we would prefer whisky or brandy. We both opted for the former and a few minutes later, a valet arrived with a decanter, glasses and a gasogene.

"This is a very fine Irish pot still whisky," said Mycroft. "Unfortunately, I believe it pales in comparison to Lord Hargreaves' Glenturret."

Unable to restrain my curiosity, I blurted out, "How could you possibly know about the Glenturret?"

"No doubt Mycroft gave him that bottle," replied Holmes.

"Well done, Sherlock," said his brother. "Now I believe you have something for me?"

With that Holmes reached into his waistcoat pocket and pulled out a large, unpolished stone. "Is that the diamond Prescott was carrying?" I asked.

"Indeed, it is," replied Mycroft. "After making some inquiries, I learned that it was stolen from a sword hilt housed in a small museum in southern France, and I have made arrangements to have it returned."

"Have you searched Lady Cox's estate?"

"We have, and we are in the process of returning pilfered treasures to their rightful owners – both private parties and museums."

"And what will you do regarding those individuals who have purchased a counterfeit?"

"We shall do absolutely nothing," replied Mycroft. "After all, this is one of those rare cases where ignorance may indeed be bliss."

"Then I believe that concludes our business here," said Holmes as he sipped his whisky.

"It certainly brings this affair to a close," said Mycroft, "as for our business, I have the feeling our paths will cross in the not-too-distant future as they have so often in the past."

"No doubt you are right," remarked Holmes, and then the conversation switched to other topics – none of which I may report here.

The next day, after we had breakfasted and were reading the morning papers, I said to Holmes, "I meant to ask Mycroft, but I am certain you will know as much as he. What is to become of Lady Cox?"

"I believe that justice will follow its course in her case. After all, we witnessed her shoot Roberts, and she would most certainly have killed us. I have to believe that she has blood on her hands from other, as yet unknown, crimes."

"The gallows?"

"That is a possibility. Consider just a few of the women who have recently been hanged – Catherine Churchill in 1879; Mary Ann Barr in 1874, Elizabeth Berry in 1887, and we cannot forget sisters Catherine Flangan and Margaret Higgins who were both hanged on the same day in 1884. I could go on, but I think you get the point. English juries take a dim view of murder – no matter who commits it.

"I should think between the machinations of Mycroft, Lestrade and the other powers that be in this matter, the trial will be a low-key affair – quite possibly the sessions will be held *in camera* – that warrants little if any attention from the press." Once again, Holmes proved prophetic and the legal proceedings against Lady Ashley Cox were carried out swiftly and secretly with no coverage from Fleet Street.

Through the eloquence of her barrister, Lady Cox managed to escape the gallows, but she was sentenced to 25 years at HM Prison Holloway. Upon learning of the sentence, Holmes seemed rather disappointed. "She murdered at least one man in cold blood, ordered the death of another, and might have killed five more. I hope the prison will be able to contain her."

After a pause, he continued, "The only bright side to this sentence that I can see is that if she should survive it, she will be too old to do much mischief when she is released."

At that point, Mrs. Hudson knocked on the door. "Come in," Holmes said across the room.

Our landlady entered rather tentatively and said, "This letter just arrived for you, Mr. Holmes. I tried to persuade the messenger to wait, but he hopped on his bicycle and sped off."

"Thank you, Mrs. Hudson," said Holmes.

Looking at me and holding up the envelope, Holmes said, "I have no idea what is in here, but if it is someone seeking an appointment, you have my word that I will put my desire for paste on hold and be here when the caller arrives."

Author's note

Most of the characters in the book are products of my imagination, but I do refer to a few historical personages such as the antiquarians Augustus Pitt Rivers and Augustus Wollaston Franks.

Just about all the artifacts mentioned in this book from the Mérode Cup to the Lewis chessmen, to the Alfred Jewel, are real and may be seen in the museums that house them. *Plique à jour* was a technique in the Middle Ages that has probably been rendered significantly easier by technology.

The forging of artifacts and paintings in the Victorian Era was a very real problem, and one that continues to plague museums and collectors, albeit to a lesser degree, today.

The South Kensington Museum, which became the Victoria and Albert Museum has its origins in the Great Exhibition of 1851. At its opening in 1852, it was known as the Museum of Manufactures. By February 1854 discussions were underway to transfer the museum to the current site on Cromwell Road, and it was renamed the South Kensington Museum.

The official opening by Queen Victoria occurred on 20 June, 1857. Her Majesty returned to lay the foundation stone of the Aston Webb building (to the left of the main entrance) on 17 May, 1899. It was during this ceremony that the name change from 'South Kensington Museum' to 'Victoria and Albert Museum' was made public. Queen Victoria's address during the ceremony was recorded in The London Gazette, and it concluded with the line, "I trust that it will remain for ages a Monument of discerning Liberality and a Source of Refinement and Progress."

Acknowledgements

I continue to maintain that writing, at least as I practice it, is a lonely task. I do most of my writing late at night when everyone else is in bed, and there is complete silence in the house. I have no idea why it works for me, but it does.

Fortunately, the task of assembling some 65,000 words has been made somewhat less onerous by the encouragement and patience of friends and family, who have continued to support me and encourage my literary endeavors.

I should be terribly remiss if I failed to thank my publisher, Steve Emecz, who makes the process painless, and Brian Belanger, whose skill as a cover designer remains unmatched.

No book is complete without a solid line edit, and Deborah Annakin Peters continues to do yeoman duty in that position, providing me with any number of invaluable suggestions, catching the Americanisms that slip in and saving me from any number of faux pas with regard to the true Mother tongue.

I also owe a considerable debt to Bob Katz, a good friend, who remains the finest Sherlockian I know. From my first efforts, he has continued to encourage me and is kind enough to read my efforts with an eye toward accuracy – both with regard to the Canon, and perhaps more importantly, to common sense.

To Francine and Richard Kitts, two more Sherlockians par excellence, for their unflagging support and encouragement.

To my brother, Edward, and my sister, Arlene, who quite often had more faith in me than I had in myself.

Finally, to all those, and there are far too many to name, whose support for my earlier efforts have made me see just what a wonderful life I have and what great people I am surrounded by. To all those who have read my earlier works, a sincere thank you.

To say that I am in the debt of all those mentioned here doesn't even begin to scratch the surface of my gratitude.

About the author

Richard T. Ryan is a native New Yorker, having been born and raised on Staten Island. He majored in English at St. Peter's College in Jersey City and pursued his graduate studies, concentrating on medieval literature, at the University of Notre Dame in Indiana.

After teaching high school and college for several years, he joined the staff of the Staten Island Advance. He worked there for nearly 30 years, rising through the ranks to become news editor. When he retired in 2016, he held the position of publications manager for that paper, although he still prefers the title, news editor.

In addition to his first novel, "The Vatican Cameos: A Sherlock Holmes Adventure," he has written "The Stone of Destiny: A Sherlock Holmes Adventure," "The Druid of Death," "The Merchant of Menace" and "Through a Glass Starkly."

He is also the author of "B Is for Baker Street (My First Sherlock Holmes Book)," which he wrote for his grandchildren, Riley Grace and Henry Robert. It is illustrated by Sophia Asbury.

He has also penned three trivia books, including "The Official Sherlock Holmes Trivia Book."

In a different medium, he can boast at having "Deadly Relations," a mystery-thriller produced off-Broadway on two separate occasions.

And if that weren't enough, he is also the very proud father of two children, Dr. Kaitlin Ryan-Smith and Michael Ryan.

He has been married for more than 43 years to his wife, Grace, and continues to marvel at her inexhaustible patience in putting up with him and his computer illiteracy. They live together with Homer, a black Lab mix, who is the real king of the Ryan castle.

He is currently at work on his seventh Holmes novel, while researching a long-delayed period piece set in the Middle Ages. After that, he may take yet another look into the tin dispatch box he purchased at auction in Scotland and see what tales remain.

Read on for an excerpt from the next Sherlock Holmes
Adventure by Richard T. Ryan

The Tower Bridge Mystery:

A Sherlock Holmes Adventure

5 August, 1889

For some odd reason, I remember every detail of that day vividly. Part of the recollection may stem from the fact that Holmes had just finished working on an adventure which I subsequently titled "The Adventure of the Naval Treaty," and I was assembling my notes on that rather memorable affair.

My wife had departed the previous day to visit relatives in Scotland, and I had taken up residence in my old room at Baker Street. It was a Monday, and the time was exactly 11:44 a.m. when I heard the front door bell ring. Whoever was calling was impatient, as the ring was repeated twice more before Mrs. Hudson had the opportunity to move from the kitchen – where she was preparing lunch for Holmes and me. Since she normally answers before even a second ring is required, I felt that the matter on which the caller had come to see Holmes must be one of some urgency.

"Someone would appear to be in quite a hurry to see you?" I said.

"Oh," remarked Holmes, who had been working at his chemistry table and concentrating so hard that he had been oblivious to the sound of the bell.

The footfalls ascending the stairs were quite rapid, and I can only assume that our caller was taking the stairs two at a time. When a heavy hand struck the door thrice in succession, Holmes, who had shifted his attention from his experiment to the sounds emanating from below after my comment, looked at me, and said, "I wonder what could possibly bring Inspector Lestrade here on a Monday and in a mood that seemingly will brook no nonsense."

"Come in, Inspector," he called across the room.

I was not surprised when Lestrade entered. I had seen Holmes perform similar feats of deduction on countless occasions. Normally not the neatest man, I must say that Lestrade looked positively disheveled as he stood there, quite obviously out of breath and out of his depth. "Thank goodness, you are here, Mr. Holmes," he wheezed. "I don't know what I should have done if you weren't."

"Take a moment to catch your breath, Inspector," I advised.

At the same time, Holmes said, "What on Earth is the matter, Lestrade? And why are you working instead of tending to your garden? I thought you were supposed to be taking a short holiday."

"I'm covering today for Inspector Finley; his son is getting married. Each inspector volunteered for one day."

"Well, you will congratulate Finley when you see him. He's a good man."

"I certainly will," replied Lestrade. "Now to the matter at hand. There has been a murder, or at least I believe there has."

"That's rather a lot to take in, and while I am in my element dealing with *apparent* contradictions, I must say this doesn't appear to be one. Either you have a murder or you do not.

"Do you have a dead body?" Holmes asked.

Lestrade nodded and then said, "Of course, we do."

"But you are uncertain of the cause of death?"

"You hit the mark there, Mr. Holmes. As far as we can tell from a cursory examination, there were no wounds on the body, but there are at least two possible causes of death which seem readily apparent."

"And have you identified these potential causes?"

"Yes, sir. Asphyxiation or possibly starvation."

"My word," I exclaimed.

"We expect to know for certain after a post mortem has been conducted, Doctor, but for the moment, it appears as though it could have been either one – possibly both in concert."

"Either way – that's an agonizing death," I offered.

"Whether he were starved to death or suffocated, it certainly constitutes murder. Where was the body found, Lestrade?"

"As you know, Mr. Holmes, they have been working on the Tower Bridge for more than three years now."

"I am well aware of that, Inspector. Given the rate of progress, I expect they will be working on it for at least three more, quite possibly longer."

"In recent weeks, the masons have been concentrating on the Southwark side tower. As there were some difficulties with that tower, apparently.

"As a result the tower on the north side of the river has languished and been vacant for nearly a month.

"At any rate, when the workers reported to the north tower this morning, one of them noticed a section of wall that seemed out of place. When they examined it, it didn't line up with the specifications, and after examining it carefully, the foreman considered the masonry to be substandard.

"He had one of the men pry out a brick; as a result, they discovered that it was more a façade than an actual section of wall. Reaching inside, the foreman felt cloth, so they decided to take down part of the section and see what it concealed. That's when they discovered the body."

"You know, Lestrade, this sounds a great deal like that short story, 'The Cask of Amontillado' by Mr. Edgar Allan Poe," I offered.

"Indeed, it does," replied Lestrade, "but that's not the strangest thing."

"There's more to this macabre tale?" asked Holmes.

"Yes, sir. The body is that of a man. If I had to guess – and given the state of the corpse, I'd just be guessing – I would say he was about six feet tall, perhaps 40 years old, clean-shaven, with a full head of very dark brown hair."

"I don't suppose anyone matching that description has been reported missing," I ventured.

"Not as far as I know, Doctor, but we are still making inquiries. So something may yet turn up."

"The proximity of the bridge to the Tower of London is rather suggestive in that it sounds as though this man might well have been a prisoner of some sort," mused Holmes, "Any idea how long he has been in there?"

"We are hoping the coroner will able to narrow it down, but as a guess, I would say at least two weeks, perhaps three."

"Tell me, Inspector, what was he wearing."

"He had on a grey suit with a proper waistcoat and dark blue cravat. However, the cravat had been removed and tied around his mouth as a gag. I should also mention that both his hands and feet were bound."

"That is rather important," remarked Holmes, adding, "It suggests that he was alive when the wall was built.

"Can you tell me anything about his boots?"

"Truth be told, I think they were black, but I really didn't take much notice of them."

"The color is immaterial. I need to see the shape they are in, for they may well tell me where this man has been. Obviously, you have a murdered man on your hands. But why come to me, when you have just discovered the body?"

"That's what I've been trying to tell you, Mr. Holmes, but you kept putting me off with all your questions."

"My apologies, Inspector," Holmes said without the least bit of contrition in his voice. Please continue."

"As you might expect, the man's wallet was missing, and he carried no papers that might help identify him that we could discover. However, tucked away in the breast pocket of his jacket was a small piece of paper that whoever killed him must have overlooked."

"And what, pray tell, did it say Inspector?"

"Printed on it in neat block letters were the words: 221B BAKER STREET."

Also from Richard Ryan

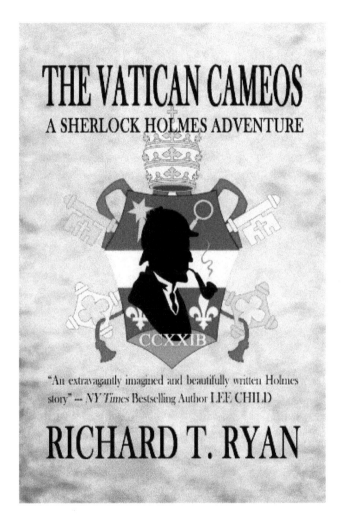

The Vatican Cameos – A Sherlock Holmes Adventure

"An extravagantly imagined and beautifully written Holmes story"
(**Lee Child**, NY Times Bestselling author, Jack Reacher series)

Also from Richard Ryan

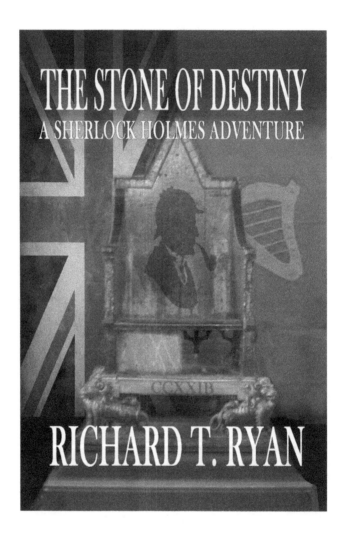

The Stone of Destiny – A Sherlock Holmes Adventure

Also from Richard Ryan

The Druid of Death – A Sherlock Holmes Adventure

"A stunning achievement"
(**Ken Bruen** Author of *The Guards* and creator of Jack Taylor)

Also from Richard Ryan

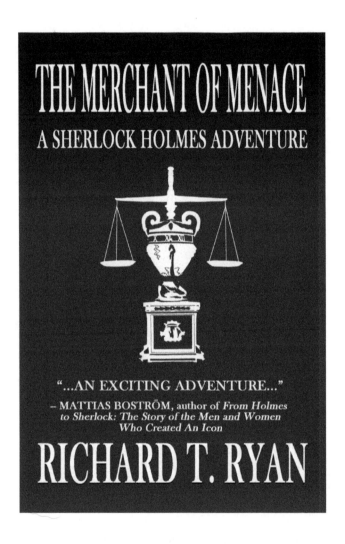

The Merchant of Menace – A Sherlock Holmes Adventure

Also from Richard Ryan

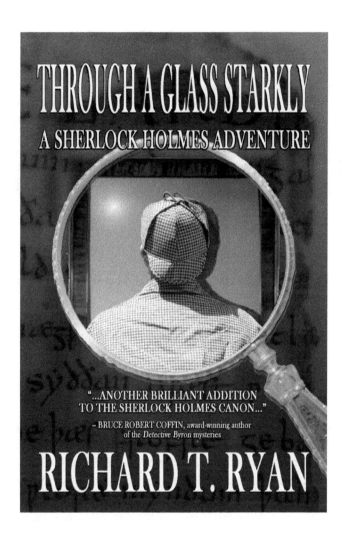

Through a Glass Starkly - A Sherlock Holmes Adventure

Also from MX Publishing

The Detective and The Woman Series

   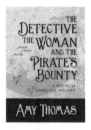

The Detective and The Woman

The Detective, The Woman and The Winking Tree

The Detective, The Woman and The Silent Hive

The Detective, The Woman and The Pirate's Bounty

"I believe the author has hit on the only type of long-term relationship possible for Sherlock Holmes and Irene Adler. The details of the narrative only add force to the romantic defects we expect in both of them and their growth and development are truly marvelous to watch. This is not a love story. Instead, it is a coming-of-age tale starring two of our favorite characters."

Philip K Jones

Also from MX Publishing

"Phil Growick's, 'The Secret Journal of Dr. Watson', is an adventure which takes place in the latter part of Holmes and Watson's lives. They are entrusted by HM Government (although not officially) and the King no less to undertake a rescue mission to save the Romanovs, Russia's Royal family from a grisly end at the hand of the Bolsheviks. There is a wealth of detail in the story but not so much as would detract us from the enjoyment of the story. Espionage, counter-espionage, the ace of spies himself, double-agents, double-crossers...all these flit across the pages in a realistic and exciting way. All the characters are extremely well-drawn and Mr. Growick, most importantly, does not falter with a very good ear for Holmesian dialogue indeed. Highly recommended. A five-star effort."
The Baker Street Society

Also from MX Publishing

The Conan Doyle Notes (The Hunt For Jack The Ripper)

"Holmesians have long speculated on the fact that the Ripper murders aren't mentioned in the Canon, though the obvious reason is undoubtedly the correct one: Even if Conan Doyle had suspected the killer's identity he'd never have considered mentioning it in the context of a fictional entertainment. Ms. Madsen's novel equates his silence with that of the dog in the night-time, assuming that Conan Doyle did know who the Ripper was but chose not to say – which, of course, implies that good old stand-by, the government cover-up. It seems unlikely to me that the Ripper was anyone famous or distinguished, but fiction is not fact, and "The Conan Doyle Notes" is a gripping tale, with an intelligent, courageous and very likable protagonist in DD McGil."
The Sherlock Holmes Society of London

Also from MX Publishing

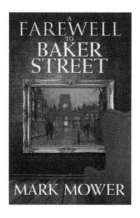

Farewell to Baker Street

Here is a collection of five previously unknown cases from the astonishing career of the consulting detective and his ever-loyal partner. An Affair of the Heart demonstrates the critical interplay between the two men which made their partnership so memorable and endearing. The Curious Matter of the Missing Pearmain is a classic locked-room mystery, while The Case of the Cuneiform Suicide Note sees Dr. Watson using his expert knowledge in helping to solve the mystery surrounding the death of an academic. In A Study in Verse the pair assists the Birmingham City Police in a complicated case of robbery which leads them towards a new and dangerous adversary. And to complete the collection, we have The Trimingham Escapade, the very last case the pair enjoyed together, which neatly showcases the inestimable talents of Sherlock Holmes.

About MX Publishing

MX Publishing is the world's largest specialist Sherlock Holmes publisher, with over four hundred titles and two hundred authors creating the latest in Sherlock Holmes fiction and non-fiction.

Our largest project is The MX Book of New Sherlock Holmes which is the world's largest collection of new Sherlock Holmes Stories – with over two hundred contributors including NY Times bestsellers Lee Child, Nicholas Meyer, Lindsay Faye and Kareem Abdul Jabar. The collection has raised over $85,000 for Stepping Stones School for children with learning disabilities.

Learn more at www.mxpublishing.com

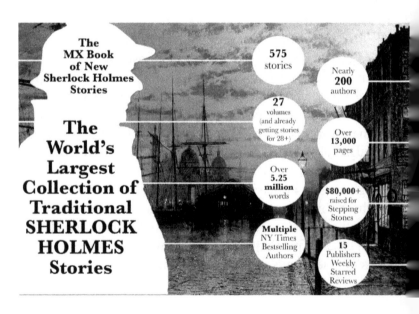

(as of May 2021 – more volumes on the way!)

Lightning Source UK Ltd.
Milton Keynes UK
UKHW021116201021
392517UK00004B/42